REPOSSESSION

Nicola Thorne

This first world edition published in Great Britain 1996 by
SEVERN HOUSE PUBLISHERS LTD of
9–15 High Street, Sutton, Surrey SM1 1DF.
First published in the USA 1996 by
SEVERN HOUSE PUBLISHERS INC. of
595 Madison Avenue, New York, NY 10022.

British Library Cataloguing in Publication Data

Thorne, Nicola
  Repossession
  1. English fiction – 20th century
  I. Title
  823.9'14 [F]

  ISBN 0-7278-4931-X

Typeset by Palimpsest Book Production Limited,
Polmont, Stirlingshire, Scotland.
Printed and bound in Great Britain by
Hartnolls Ltd, Bodmin, Cornwall.

REPOSSESSION

Contents

PART I

For Better, For Worse

Chapter One

There was an eerie silence inside the house, as though something terrible had happened there. Helen Tempest, feeling the goose pimples rise on her arms, rubbed them vigorously with her hands and stood hugging herself. Then she shook her head.

The silence was broken by the two children who suddenly rushed indoors from their inspection of the garden. They were followed by their father, a broad smile on his face.

"Like it?" he asked Helen.

"Well there's nothing actually *wrong* . . ."

Bringing up the rear of the procession, which had trooped in from the garden, the estate agent carefully closed the front door.

"There's nothing *wrong* with it at all, Mrs Tempest. It's in excellent condition. The previous owners, the Beckets, were professional people."

While he was enumerating the many accomplishments, professional and personal, of the former owners, Helen continued to rub her hands up and down her arms puzzled and disturbed about her reaction to a perfectly ordinary detached house some thirty years old.

It formed part of an estate built on top of a hill not far from the Dorset village of Tip Hollow. All around there were beautiful views of the Blackmore Vale, Hardy country. At the foot of the hill wound a broad stream, crossed by a narrow bridge to reach the village.

It was a very far cry from Worcester Park in Surrey, a

suburb of tree-lined streets and boxed houses of almost monotonous uniformity.

It was a sizeable, four-bedroomed house. A lounge-dining room ran from front to back. There was a wide hall into which ran a staircase; a kitchen, morning room and utility room; a garage and an eighth of an acre of garden in need of some attention.

"Some repossessed houses are left in an awful state," the agent went on chattily. "This—"

"Repossessed!" The goose pimples returned to her arms, the feeling of ethereal chill to her body. "Did you say this house is *repossessed*?"

Nervously the agent consulted the particulars in his hand. Then he glanced uneasily at John Tempest, who was standing at the front window looking at the view.

"I did *tell* you it was repossessed, Mr Tempest."

John airily waved a hand.

"I forgot—"

"But how could you forget a thing like that?" Helen burst out angrily. "A house that has been forcefully taken away—"

"They hadn't been here very long . . ." the agent chipped in as if that were a mitigating factor.

"Helen it's ideal." John tried to hide his impatience.

"But if you know they weren't happy here."

"How do you *know* they weren't happy here?"

"As far as I remember he was an architect." The agent consulted his notes again. "The practice got into difficulties."

The children, who had disappeared upstairs, came running down, their faces glowing.

"Mum, upstairs is simply *super*!" Meg reached out to grab her mother by the hand. "Do come and have a look."

Reluctantly Helen allowed herself to be led upstairs. Yes the rooms were spacious and the position a good one. In the Home Counties the same place would have

4

been expected to fetch thousands more. The reserve price expected at auction was £65,000. Imagine a four-bedroomed house for that price near London?

Downstairs the agent droned on telling John about the schools, the facilities in the nearby town, Yeovil. Poole and Bournemouth were not very far away.

"What *is* it Mum?" Meg screwed up her trusting little face and looked anxiously at her mother. "It's the nicest we've seen."

Helen rubbed her arms again, looking round. But now she felt different. The goose pimply feeling had gone.

Perhaps it was all in her imagination.

They had given up ten days to house-hunting and the house on Tip Hollow Hill was by far the nicest they'd seen, the best value for the expected asking price. The estate was a small one of executive houses built in the boom of the Sixties. As they shut the garden gate the family turned and stood for a moment gazing at it.

It was true that very little needed to be done.

"The auction," the agent said, "is on Thursday week. If you're interested you haven't very long to have a survey done. You know the rules of auction don't you?"

There was no problem. They were being relocated by John's firm and were cash buyers.

Helen said, "You didn't tell *me* the house was repossessed."

"I forgot." John had his eyes on the second row of books he was taking down from the shelves. Already they had started packing. The idea was to go into a hotel or rent until they had found a house. John's insurance company, where he was to be branch manager, was already opening in Yeovil. For him it was an exciting, stimulating challenge.

John Tempest was thirty-seven. He had joined the

company at the age of eighteen and diligently worked his way up, taking all the insurance exams, doing well. He was moderately ambitious and, because of the nature of his job, concerned about security, careful about money almost to the point of meanness.

"I can't *believe* you forgot." Helen stood at the bottom of the ladder staring up at him with bright, accusing eyes. John looked down at her.

"What does it matter?"

"I think it matters that people were unhappy there."

"Don't be silly." John, with an armful of books, mostly on insurance, banking and military history, which was his hobby, got carefully down from the ladder. "From what the agent told us they were glad to get out of it."

"That's what *he* says. How can he know?"

"Is there any reason not to believe him?" John carefully removed his spectacles and wiped his brow. It was August. Hot. No time to be moving really. Yet he was eager to be at his new post after all these years as a junior, an assistant, finally one of the many deputies at the large branch that had moved to purpose-built premises in Worcester Park from the City of London a decade before. Now they were talking of relocating even further afield, and the West Country was a possibility for the new head office if the series of branch offices opening there was successful.

Hot outside in August, but inside the temperature rose too. John perched on top of the steps and, replacing his spectacles, put his handkerchief in his pocket and gazed calmly at his wife.

"Helen you know this move is for the best. It's promotion for me. It's—" he gesticulated wildly with his arms – "it's leaving this rather cramped house and moving to a nice part of the country. The schools are good, the children will flourish."

"They're flourishing perfectly well here." Helen plopped

6

down on the sofa opposite him, her features rigid. "There's just one person you're leaving out of all this. Me."

"I am thinking of you—"

"Of how hard it will be for me to get a job," she went on as if not listening.

"But you don't *know* it will be hard. Besides, with my increase in salary it won't be necessary."

"Oh you just want me to be a stay-at-home wife do you?"

"Isn't that what you'd like?" Agitatedly, John pushed his spectacles up his nose.

"No it isn't. I like going out to work, having my own money. I've acquired the skills that I need for a good secretarial job."

"Those you can use in Yeovil."

"I don't know that I particularly want to work in Yeovil."

"Yeovil looked like a nice place to me. Good shops, yet in the heart of the country."

Helen made a noise that was a cross between a snigger and a laugh.

"You can hardly compare Yeovil with the West End."

"The West End doesn't nestle in the middle of gorgeous countryside. On the contrary."

"The 'gorgeous countryside' as you call it doesn't have so many part-time jobs. Unemployment is higher in the West Country than in any part of the UK."

John sighed heavily and gazed at the floor. He was a patient man. In the insurance business you could hardly not be and yet . . .

"What *is* it you want Helen?"

"I would like *you* to have consulted *me* before you accepted the job."

"I thought you'd be thrilled. It never occurred to me you'd want to discuss it."

"Talked it over . . . weighed up the pros and cons.

Instead you come home and brightly announce 'we're moving'."

"I *thought* you'd be delighted. I really did."

"Then when you found out I wasn't delighted it didn't stop you. And the children. They're happy in their school. All their friends are round here. They're doing well. I was happy in a nice part-time job. All my friends are round here too."

"So you want me to pack it in? Reject the job?" John clenched his jaw in a stubborn line. "I mean if we had talked it over would it have made any difference? Would you really have me turn down a job that meant managerial status and a greatly increased salary?" As she continued to stare at him without replying he flung his arms helplessly into the air. "Anyway why bring it up now? We're moving out next week."

Too late. Helen stood at the sink looking out of the kitchen window until the smell of burnt toast made her spin round and rescue it from the toaster. This was one of the things she would certainly not be taking with her: a toaster that stuck, burning the toast.

Well, rationally, there was a lot to be said for moving. They had been here since the birth of Meg eleven years before when Icumen Life had transferred its mammoth insurance operations from the City. Jake was then three years old and in those days – sometimes it seemed a lifetime ago now – Helen had been quite happy to be a housewife and mother, still enjoying married life, the security of a home, a loving husband in a safe job.

Helen had left school at sixteen with good O levels, trained as a secretary and worked in a bank. She met John at a dance when she was nineteen. She had lived all her life with her parents in Gunnersbury, not far from the river Thames, and John had lived all of his with his parents and two brothers one stop up the line at Turnham Green.

It was a conventional courtship. Saturday nights out

with friends, Sunday on the river in the summer, various outdoor or indoor activities in winter. A life lived very much with other people; seldom alone. John's father was a salesman, Helen's a draughtsman. Both of their mothers did part-time jobs, one in a store, one in a works' canteen. Their backgrounds were similar, their interests were alike. They married two years after they met, and a year after that Jake was born.

For a year they lived in a rented flat near Helen's parents. It was useful to have her mother on hand when she was pregnant. But then she was used to having her mother on hand all the time. In many ways Helen, as an only child, was Mummy's girl.

Then came the move to Worcester Park, the excitement of their first house, a semi in a pleasant tree-lined road about ten minutes from the new building. At first John came home to lunch, but not long after Meg was born he stopped. For one thing he travelled around quite a bit selling insurance and then, as his responsibilities increased, he either had a sandwich at his desk or a ploughman's and a pint of beer at the pub with the boys.

It was when she had to cope on her own with a small, fractious toddler and a baby with colic, that the joy began to go out of Helen's marriage and after that it became drudgery. Her mother was no longer at hand; her father had taken early retirement. As a couple her parents had often visited and loved Spain, and decided on a whim to retire there, to Torremolinos where they'd had so many happy holidays. Helen missed them dreadfully, especially her mum.

Then when Jake was eight and Meg five and starting infant school, Helen began to feel the yearning for the freedom she had lost. She looked around for diversion: her own part-time job, her own small route to independence. But secretarial skills had advanced considerably since she last worked in an office. It was the advent of word processors, faxes and laser printers. She retrained and got a part-time job as a receptionist and then, as her new skills improved, as a secretary for a builder in Worcester Park. And there she had remained, quite happily, ever since.

She had her circle of girlfriends. She went to one or two classes during the day and sometimes in the evenings. Her life and John's grew subtly but increasingly apart, their interests differing, their friends no longer in common.

But weren't most people's marriages like that? Wasn't that why women talked about men all the time and men, well, everyone knew they never discussed personal matters. They talked either jobs, sport or the state of the nation. Anyway men didn't make close friendships like women did.

Helen spread Flora and low calorie jam on her toast – she was worried about her figure, now inclined to plumpness – and after pouring water on to her Nescafé drew the cup towards her and opened the *Daily Mail*. There was a tap on the kitchen door and before she could call "come in" the door opened and Pauline Burns, her best friend, stood looking at her, her expression crestfallen.

"Whatever is the matter?" Helen asked, looking up from her paper. "Your face is a picture."

"I just can't bear to think of you going." Pauline collapsed into a chair at the other side of the table and looked as though she was going to cry.

Helen and Pauline had been good friends for a long time. Their children were friends at school – Pauline had a daughter the same age as Meg – and as Pauline was recently divorced she depended desperately on the friend who had seen her through all her recent traumas.

Helen stretched out a hand.

"You'll come and stay."

"It's not the same."

"Don't think *I* like it."

"Then why are you going? Didn't you have *any* say in the matter?"

"Not really." Helen, lips pursed, rose and spooned Nescafé into a mug for Pauline. "Of course John has a point," she added, glancing over her shoulder. "It is a promotion, more money. He couldn't have got a senior managerial job staying where he was."

"I thought he was a manager?"

"I mean his own branch."

"But you're so settled, and your job."

"Please don't talk about it Pauline." Helen passed her a mug of coffee and sat down wearily.

"You don't look as though you've been sleeping."

"I haven't."

"It's that house isn't it? You don't really like it."

"Well we haven't got it yet. Hopefully someone will pay more at the auction than John wants to pay."

"Mind you," Pauline, who had seen it before, once again drew the brochure towards her, "it is *ever* so nice. Big too. You'll be able to have another baby," she concluded with a giggle. "Just like the Queen."

"How do you mean 'just like the Queen'?"

"Well wasn't there ten years between Anne and . . . Andrew was it, or Edward? I can't remember."

"I can't either. I always mix them up anyway. I certainly *shan't* be having another baby."

"I would have thought there was a lot of property about." Pauline idly turned the pages of the estate agent's brochure. "Why did you have to have this particular one?"

"Because it suits John. It is in a nice village not too far from Yeovil. It has a cricket club and a football pitch and a nice pub and, of course, as a forced sale we shall get it cheap. Economy, as you know, means such a lot to John. Oh I liked the house, the locality . . ." Helen felt that peculiar feeling on her skin again as if something were crawling all over it. "I can't explain. It's *stupid* . . ."

"Hundreds of people have had their houses repossessed, hundreds of thousands—"

"Oh I know." Helen shook her head. "I can't explain it. It just didn't seem right, as if there was still unhappiness somehow locked within those walls. Well anyway," she looked at the clock and jumped up, "the auction's on Thursday, so this time next week we'll know."

"Going at £72,000." The auctioneer looked up, his hand on the gavel. "Any advance on £72,000?"

John looked nervously round. As the auctioneer banged down his gavel there was a rustle among the audience who fell to studying their auction sheets.

"£72,000," John hissed to Helen. "At this rate we're not going to get it. I thought prices were supposed to be low?" Helen studied the details on the sheet before her. It was a larger house than the one on Tip Hollow Hill, but in many ways they were identical. Maybe it was a bit nearer the town but that was all. In any event it had been sold way above the estimated price. Suddenly it seemed that her heart rose with hope. John would *never* pay that kind of price for a house.

"14 Tip Hollow Hill," the auctioneer announced briskly. "Here we have a very nice detached house in good condition and a nice location, with nearby amenities and country views. Can I start the bidding at £65,000 please?" He looked expectantly up but no hands were raised. "£64,000? Will anyone bid £64,000?"

Again silence. "£62,000?" the auctioneer said, a note of desperation entering his voice. "Will anyone start me at £60,000 for this fine, detached house in prime position overlooking the ancient village of Tip Hollow?"

Again there was silence. The crowd began to murmur among themselves, some to stir restlessly.

"£20,000," a voice called out from the centre of the hall. "I'll give you £20,000."

"Come now, sir. Be sensible, please!" The auctioneer now had a trace of impatience in his voice. Normally he

12

expected to dispose of a house at a repossession sale in a few seconds. He glanced at his watch.

"£35,000," John said suddenly in a firm voice.

"£35,000, thank you sir." The auctioneer looked at him pointedly. "Do I have any advance on £35,000?" Once again he looked around. "Come on, this is a very fine house built in 1963, left by the previous owners in excellent condition with a well-laid garden in an eighth of an acre of land. Any advance on £35,000?" No one bid. The gavel rose in the air. The auctioneer looked around and then at John. "You sir, at £35,000. A bargain if I may say so." He shook his head as if in incomprehension at such inconsistency in prices and then went on to the next property.

Helen could feel John trembling beside her, his fist clenching and unclenching. The estimate had been £65,000, quite cheap for a house of this standard compared with London prices. And yet he had got it for £30,000 less. It seemed incredible.

"Come on, quickly," he said getting up and grabbing her hand. "Before they change their minds."

The formalities were soon over, the deposit paid. It was much easier to buy a house at auction than the usual method. The offer was binding. People who repossessed houses wanted to get some money, any money, to offset the debt which would never be fully paid anyway.

"I can't believe my luck." John emerged into the sunlit streets of Yeovil from the auction room. "*£35,000*. Now there's no need to get a mortgage."

John would love that. No need to get a mortgage, no debt. Outright ownership. Helen looked at him rather contemptuously.

"Well come on, let's celebrate," John said. "Fancy a nice lunch?"

"Not really. I'm not hungry."

"Oh come *on* love." He took her arm and pressed her

close to him. "Cheer up. We've got a house. Aren't you excited?"

Helen didn't reply and silently they walked up the street into the dining room of the *Three Cheoghs* hotel at the top of the hill.

"Now dear what will you have?" John asked studying the menu. "Have what you like, no expense spared."

They scarcely ever ate out. John always thought it was a waste of money. He didn't think it was a waste of money if someone paid for him, business lunches or the odd invitation from friends to eat in a restaurant, few and far between because the hospitality was never reciprocated.

Helen looked at the menu which normally would have tempted her. Instead she felt slightly nauseous.

"I'll have a salad," she said at last, firmly closing the menu and placing it on the table in front of her.

John looked up in surprise.

"Only a salad! Oh come on Helen. You can do better than that. Have a steak. Have fillet steak."

"It's all I want. Thank you," she added firmly.

"And a glass of wine?" he added with a smile as though encouraging an invalid to take her medicine.

A glass of wine, she agreed, would be very nice. Very welcome. She almost gulped it down when it came.

"I can't understand you Helen," John said peevishly after he had given their order. Ham salad for Helen, a mixed grill with chips for him. John was lean and could eat chips. Helen, these days, always careful with her figure. "I would have expected you to be happy and excited. Instead of which you're nothing but a misery."

Helen, close to tears, choked as she took another deep gulp of wine.

"Excited on my behalf," John went on pausing only for a moment as the dishes they had ordered were set before them. "A new job, a new life." He stopped and stared at her. "We're still under forty. We can do a *lot*

14

with our lives. With this new promotion I could make area manager. We could move in no time at all to a bigger, purpose-built house."

"You forget I had *all* my friends in Worcester Park." Helen stared apathetically at the tempting slices of thick Wiltshire ham on the plate in front of her, the dishes of enticing salads at her side.

"Oh it's *that*." John sat back with an air of relief. "I thought it was something to do with the house."

"It is *also* something to do with the house . . . as well," Helen continued after a pause. "It's not the only thing but I don't like the fact it's been repossessed. I told you that from the beginning. To me it seemed like an unhappy place. I could feel it in the walls . . ."

"Oh that *is* rubbish." John began to tuck vigorously into his mixed grill. "There's no such thing. 'Feel it in the walls'. How ridiculous!" He leaned forward staring at her accusingly. "Do you realize every house that was in the sale today was repossessed? They can't *all* be unhappy places can they? They were lapped up weren't they? A lot of satisfied buyers there today if you ask me."

"Then why was ours to *especially* cheap? Why did *no one* else bid?"

"Yes. That was a puzzle." John scratched his head. "Search me. No one wanted a property in Tip Hollow."

"They expected £65,000, we got it for *£35,000*. Thirty thousand pounds cheaper. Isn't that an awful lot compared with the other prices?"

"It was a bargain." John leaned back and took a sip from his glass, smacking his lips as he replaced it on the table. "I don't care how unhappy the place is if I can get a bargain like that," he added flippantly.

"You're unfeeling John, that's what. I think there's something wrong with that house. I tell you the place gave me goose pimples . . ." And she began to rub her arms as the familiar flesh-crawling process started all over again.

* * *

15

Dr Warner looked at Helen sympathetically, then leaned back studying her record card.

"It's understandable you should feel this depression about a move Mrs Tempest. Weepy fits, lack of energy, insomnia. It's a great upheaval in anyone's life. After all, you've been here a long time." He turned over the card, checking the date she'd first registered at the practice. "Twelve years, nearly."

"We came just before Meg was born."

"Well it *is* a very long time and maybe your husband hasn't shown you quite the sympathy you think you deserve, the understanding, is that it?"

Helen nodded, the tears beginning to well just under her eyelids again.

"Yet in a way you can understand *him*. He's got a new job; he's impatient to get started and you say you don't really like the house?"

Helen shook her head feeling too foolish to say why.

"Then why did you buy it? Surely he could have accommodated you on that."

"We got it very cheap." Her lip started to tremble. "It was repossessed."

"Ah!" Dr Warner nodded. "They *do* go very cheap, alas. It's a sad world isn't it?"

"But it was extremely cheap, well below the price it was expected to fetch. No one else bid for it."

"Then you were very lucky. Try to look on the bright side." The doctor smiled reassuringly at her. "That's one bit of good news anyway."

"Even then I didn't want it. There was something about it."

"Old place, was it?" The doctor looked sympathetic. "Old rectory in the country?"

"Oh no, it's quite modern. On a small estate."

"Oh well, no ghosts then. I don't suppose you've very much to worry about Mrs Tempest. Just getting used to the place I expect." He paused and, pulling his pad

16

towards him, started writing out a prescription which he tore from the pad and handed to her.

"Now I've given you two lots of pills; a very mild tranquillizer, and an anti-depressant. Just to get you through the period of moving." He pressed the bell on his desk and stood up. "It's an upheaval for most people, even those like your husband who look forward to it. People number it among the severe traumas, like divorce and death." He put out his hand. "As soon as you've registered with a new doctor in your area we'll send on your records. Don't be afraid to ask for a repeat prescription. And the very best of luck to you and your family Mrs Tempest. Lots of joy in your new home."

Joy in your new home. Helen sat in the car for a long time after John had gone to let the removal men in. They had followed the van down from Worcester Park, along the M3, and finally, the A303. She and John had been very quiet during the trip. Helen was desperately tired, because of the pills, she supposed, as much as anything. But still they didn't lessen the anguish of saying goodbye to her friends, finally shutting the door of a house where, on the whole, they'd been happy.

She felt she was exchanging happiness for unhappiness. And still she didn't quite know why.

As soon as the car stopped outside the house in Tip Hollow Hill the children burst through the gate and ran up the garden path, getting to the front door well before their father, but they had to wait anxiously until he produced the key.

Helen sat watching him fiddle for the key, say something to make them laugh, and then he held open the door while the children ran in. She could see the light hallway, the staircase, through to the kitchen and out of the window at the back of the house.

Carpets chosen when they were last in Yeovil had been laid in their absence, and a fresh coat of magnolia paint applied throughout. It really hadn't needed decorating, but there were always a few holes in the walls, marks where there had been mirrors or pictures. John wasn't very good at DIY although it offended his principles to spend too much on decorating. The carpet, needless to say, had been very cheap.

She wondered where John would keep his wretched wall maps of the battles of the English Civil War on which he was an expert. In Worcester Park they had been all over the house; in the hall, up the stairs, even one in the loo. Well here she was going to put her foot down. She was going to have prints of pretty country scenes, maybe original paintings by local artists, rather than maps of events, and gory ones at that, 300 years old.

Seeing the open door, the stretch of country through the kitchen window, the removal men unfastening the great doors at the back of their van and beginning to unload what was, after all, familiar furniture, made her feel better, almost cheerful. Maybe the pills were working or, maybe, it was because she had accepted that now they had finally moved; or maybe she had said goodbye to the past or, maybe, it was because it was a lovely day and it was very nice after all to be in the country, such beautiful country at that. Who could say?

She got out of the car and undid the boot to be greeted by a plaintive whine. Skittles the cat crouched at the back of her wire basket, eyes opaque with fear. They had stopped on the way down at regular intervals to make sure she was all right, but the paper at the bottom of the basket was soaked with urine and Helen's heart went out in pity to this beloved companion. Murmuring soothing noises she gently drew out the basket and put a finger through the bars.

"There there," she said, "There there!"

Skittles gazed at her suspiciously for a moment and then, arching her back, sidled up to the side of the cage

18

and rubbed her cheek against Helen's finger. Momentarily, Helen was tempted to take her out, but decided against it. If Skittles dashed away out of fright, goodness knew when she would be found again. You had to keep them inside a new abode for at least seven days, or so she'd read.

The first job seemed to be to change the paper in Skittles' basket and this she did using a copy of *The Times* that John had, not unnaturally, not yet found time to read. Serve him right. She opened the gate of the cage making sure the cat, by now a little mollified and subdued, did not escape and changed the paper, stuffing the used sheets in a plastic bag and gently smoothing the fresh newspaper at the bottom of the cage.

"Won't be long now," she whispered, stroking the head of the grey tabby. "Just a few more minutes, darling." Then she closed the gate, picked up the basket and turned resolutely towards the house.

Their new home, for better or worse.

She stood aside with a smile to let two of the removal men stagger in with the heavy settee.

"Put it by the window," she instructed them. There was a large picture window that overlooked the valley, the hollow of the hill which was the tip. Neat really. Tip Hollow. Quite a pretty name. She was about to turn and follow them when she noticed that in the garden opposite a woman, apparently intent on gardening, was in reality following every movement.

Helen paused and stared at her and the woman, abandoning pretence and with her gardening fork in her hand, stood up and came to the gate of her own house which was almost a replica of the Tempest's, with one or two insignificant differences to justify the architect's claim that each house was different. Basically they were all the same, pretty, modern houses made of Ham stone quarried only a few miles away.

The woman would seem to be in her mid fifties, lean with a tanned face and blonde, streaked hair. She had blue eyes and her smile was friendly as she leaned over the gate.

"How do you do? Welcome to Tip Hollow. I'm Muriel Forbes."

"Helen Tempest," Helen said, hastily putting the cat basket down and crossing the road to seize the proffered hand.

"I'm so sorry I missed you when you came to look at the house. I've been away." She paused awkwardly and looked across the road. "I hope you'll be very happy here."

"Oh I'm sure we shall." As Skittles started to miaow plaintively Helen recrossed the road and stooped to retrieve the basket, Muriel following her.

"Someone said you were from London."

"Worcester Park in Surrey. On the outskirts really."

"This will be a big change."

"Oh yes."

"Tell me, have you got tea, milk? Can I help in any way?"

"That's very kind of you but," Helen jerked her head in the direction of the house, "I think everything's organized."

"Well, pop in for a drink when you're settled." Muriel's eyes travelled across Helen's shoulders and seemed to linger on the house. "It will be nice to have neighbours again."

Helen, who had already turned round, turned back. "How long is it since they moved out?"

"Not long really."

"Oh" Helen wondered how long 'not long' was.

"Yes. I didn't know them very well. No one did. They kept themselves to themselves. Of course what happened was very unfortunate."

"What *happened*?" Helen nearly tipped up the cat basket and Skittles complained loudly as once again she was put on the pavement.

"Well you know, you must know," Muriel looked to her right and left as if fearing the presence of an eavesdropper, "the house was repossessed."

"Oh yes." Helen picked the cat basket up again. "It rather put me off it.

"I hear you got it at a bargain price." A knowing look crossed Muriel's face. "Remarkably low."

"Yes we did. We wondered why no one else bid."

Muriel scratched the prong of her fork along the top of the gate, avoiding Helen's eyes. "Well, some people don't like that kind of thing do they? They think it's unlucky. And in some ways it's been an unlucky house. As far as I can tell no one has ever seemed to settle there. Odd, isn't it? And no one ever seems to know why. Maybe that's why no one else bid at the auction. Bad news gets around. Still," her frown vanished, face once again wreathed in smiles as she looked Helen in the eyes, "I don't actually *believe* in that kind of thing myself and you're such a nice, normal kind of family I'm sure you'll bring good luck to the place."

Chapter Two

Helen lay on her back, staring at the ceiling, the tall shadows made by the trees outlined against the moon. It was all very still. But then the countryside was very still. As a woman born and brought up in the suburbs of the Metropolis you were accustomed to background noise. You only missed it when it wasn't there; realized that, somehow, you were always aware of it, traffic humming away in the background, especially the busy A3 bypass out of London which had only been a few blocks away.

Here there was silence at night. Dead silence punctuated every now and then by the unfamiliar hooting of an owl or the agonized screech of a night animal as it found, or was found by, its prey. There was the bellowing of a cow when it had lost its calf; the bleat of a sheep maybe because its lambs too had been taken away, probably for slaughter. Nature could be very cruel. It was quite wrong to say it was always beautiful. You only realized it once you actually lived in the country.

Beside her John tossed in his sleep. He was worn out at night; the job had proved bigger than he thought, more taxing and demanding. He left at eight every morning dropping the children off at school on the way. They got the school bus home, but he didn't get back until seven, sometimes eight. A twelve-hour day. He realized how spoiled he had been before. But opening a new office meant so much extra responsibility; things you hadn't thought of before they happened to you.

It had been a very difficult, unsettling time and in many ways, oddly enough, John had come out of it worse. There were so many additional duties he thought he would enjoy but, instead, found rather frightening and formidable. The silence of the night. Helen put her hands behind her head and sighed. Yes, it *had* been a difficult month. Moving home after twelve years was no joke. There was also a change in her lifestyle. There was only one car and, apart from that, a bus that ran daily to Yeovil. One bus a day! Quite impossible at the moment to think of a second car, even a run-about second-hand one.

Muriel Forbes was friendly but she was often away. Just now she was in Scotland. She was a retired schoolteacher who had a number of interests which either took her away to conferences here and abroad, or to visit many friends and relations scattered around the country. The other neighbours they had not yet got to know, not well enough anyway to cadge a casual lift. One had to be so careful with the first impression one made on people. Didn't want to owe them favours.

Helen was a woman used to shops, tubes, buses, all amenities within walking distance. In Tip Hollow there was a village store which was also the post office and a small repair garage with a petrol pump.

She turned restlessly in bed and gazed at the illuminated dial of the clock. Nearly two. At seven the whole household sprang to life. She closed her eyes, but her mind remained wide awake, active.

Still, in many ways it hadn't been as bad as at first she had feared. The house no longer held any terrors for her. Once they had their own familiar furniture and possessions about them it had seemed to lose its chill, its sadness. The countryside around was of an awesome beauty; rich, rolling luxurious hills and pasture land, well fed animals grazing contentedly in fields.

There was an awful lot to do in the house and that was before she had time to turn her attention to the garden.

She hadn't a clue about gardening and it was quite fun to take one's first tentative steps towards discovering more. She'd acquired some catalogues, bought an enormous tome on gardening and found that she turned first to the gardening column in the daily paper.

Somewhere an owl hooted. Then it was almost oppressively silent . . .

All too soon it seemed the shrill sound of the alarm woke her again, and a new day began.

Later that day Helen, after her usual light lunch, sat down to watch the day's episode of *Neighbours* and afterwards, noticing that Muriel's car had parked outside her house opposite, went to the front door and stood on the doorstep watching as Muriel unpacked the boot.

"Need any help?" she called, going down the path to the gate, whereupon Muriel turned and smiled at her.

"Oh Helen! No thanks."

"Had a good trip?"

"Oh marvellous. Have you ever been to Scotland?"

Helen smiled and shook her head. "Chance would be a fine thing!"

"Well you really must go. Maybe one day when the children are off your hands," she concluded in the tone of an erstwhile schoolteacher who understood only too well the problems of parents of young children. "*Heavenly* at this time of the year."

"Come and have a cup of coffee," Helen suggested.

"Well that would be lovely; but I haven't had lunch." Muriel paused. "I thought a pub snack—"

"I'll make you a sandwich. Will that be enough?"

"That's awfully sweet of you, Helen. Really there's no need—"

"It's no trouble I assure you. Frankly I'd be glad of the company."

Muriel appeared to hesitate, consulted her watch, seemed on the point of refusing and then, changing her mind, slammed down the car boot and walked across the road. She wore jeans, a striped cotton man's shirt, and looked quite tanned, probably from walking on the Scottish hills.

The two women went into the Tempest house and Muriel sat at the kitchen table while Helen quickly prepared sandwiches and heated up the percolator.

"I bet you're tired," Helen said glancing over her shoulder. "Did you drive down in one day?"

"I stayed overnight in Cheltenham. Tell me, how are you settling in? I feel bad that I keep on popping off. But this is the time of year I make a lot of visits."

"Well that's not your fault." Helen deftly put the sandwich before her and poured coffee. "We're settling in well."

Muriel looked around her. "You seemed to have doubts about the house."

"Oh that was silly." Helen nonchalantly waved a hand. "You know I didn't like the idea that it had been repossessed, that the previous people had been unhappy here."

"Oh I think the Beckets would have been unhappy *anywhere*," Muriel said with a mouthful of sandwich.

"Oh really?"

"Yes they were that kind of family. Always rowing."

"*Really?*"

"The walls positively reverberated with the sound of discord. Disharmony I would say rather than unhappiness prevailed here."

"What did he do?" Helen sat down opposite stirring her coffee.

"He was an architect. The firm went bust and he lost his job." Muriel looked vague. "They were OK but I never got to know them very well. As a family they were not unlike you, with children of the same age, oh and a cat." She looked round. "Where's your cat?"

"She's always off somewhere. I mean she'll turn up,

but she's in her element in the country. All those voles and field mice to say nothing of the poor birds. I'll have to get a large bell and put it round her neck."

Muriel laughed, dusted her hands and drained her coffee.

"I must finish clearing the car." She stood up. "Thank you very much, Helen. It's nice to have a neighbour like you. I don't think Sue Becket ever asked me in for coffee all the time she was here. Mind you it wasn't long."

"How long?" Helen leaned earnestly across the table.

"One year? Two? She also had a miscarriage while she was here. In many ways she *was* rather an unhappy woman, come to think of it."

"What sort of age?"

"About the same as you I would think." Muriel looked at her and smiled. "How's your husband settling down in his job?"

"I think he's finding it harder than he expected." Helen followed her to the front door. "He's had some of his cockiness knocked out of him."

"Oh I do hope you settle. It's so nice having you here." Muriel looked around. "People tend to keep themselves to themselves here. I hardly know a soul. You can't blame them I suppose. Most of the women seem to work. They go off with their husbands in the morning to Yeovil or Dorchester and don't reappear until nightfall. At weekends they play golf or go shopping. Some work in the garden. I find them rather remote and a bit snobby.

"You see a few years ago these houses were in the high income bracket. It's only the recession that reduced them in price," she paused, "and this, as you know, was repossessed. You got a bargain. But that's not your fault. You were lucky. I think this house is lucky for you, not unlucky." Muriel stood up and prepared to take her departure looking towards the door and the clock on the wall. "My goodness look at the *time*!"

The two women walked together to the front door

where Muriel stopped and said they must both come to dinner. Helen said they'd love to and then stood and watched her as, with a wave, Muriel trotted down the path towards the gate, a trim erect figure, who had been head of history at a large girls' school and had taken early retirement after the school closed for lack of pupils in the recession.

Yet, despite all her toing and froing, her visits to friends, old students, various relations dotted around the country, Helen felt that Muriel was essentially a lonely woman. After all, why had she moved to this rather isolated spot in the middle of nowhere where she had no friends? No explanation there.

The place was surrounded by mysteries, really. Looking up she saw a giant cloud hovering, promising rain.

She turned back into the house again feeling decidedly uneasy.

That night Skittles didn't come home, nor did she the following night, and Helen fell once again into the grip of anxiety.

"Skittles has gone missing," she said to John as they drank their morning tea from the Teasmade at a quarter to seven prior to rousing the children. When she went downstairs to get the milk there had still been no sign of Skittles, and she went back upstairs with a heavy heart. "I think we should have kept her in longer."

"We've been here nearly two months." John had his eyes on breakfast TV and seemed unperturbed by the disappearance of the family cat. "She'll be all right. Maybe got a boyfriend." He slewed his eyes round and smiled at Helen.

"She's been spayed."

"I know but you can still fall in love, can't you?" John in fact had had a vasectomy, so perhaps he was making a point.

They'd had Skittles three years. She was really Meg's

27

cat, but the one who looked after her and perhaps cared for her best was Helen.

"I shall be very upset if she's lost," Helen said. "I shall feel responsible."

Nicholas Wichell came on to read the seven o'clock news and after listening to the headlines John got out of bed. There was an *en suite* bathroom to the master bedroom – another factor considered when buying the house – and Helen, after making the first of what would be several calls to waken the children, lay back in bed listening to him whistling under the shower; muttering to himself while he shaved. This was despite the fact that he left the door half open so that he could hear the TV.

After the stillness of the night there was so much sound in the morning. Too much. Today she had the suspicion of a headache, and she knew she was deeply worried about the cat. It seemed so unfair to bring poor Skittles to this beautiful, remote part of the country from suburbia and then lose her. It seemed all wrong.

John came into the bedroom towelling himself and made his way across to the bedside table to retrieve his spectacles. He looked severely at the clock.

"Have you called the children, Helen?"

"Yes."

"Are they up?"

"I don't know. Why don't you go and see? I've got a headache."

She flicked off the TV and snuggled her head into the pillows again. "Maybe for once this morning you could make the breakfast."

"I'd gladly make the breakfast," John said peevishly, "if *you'd* be kind enough to give me advance notice. If you'd told me you had a headache half an hour ago."

"I didn't have a headache half an hour ago."

John went out of the door and she could hear him banging on the doors of the children's bedrooms.

"Please get up, your mother's not well and it's late."

"Oh dear!" Helen heaved aside the duvet and dangled her legs over the side of the bed, rubbing a hand across her brow. She sat there for a moment, head in her hands.

"I'll get the breakfast," she called. "The head's not too bad."

"You can always go to bed again after we've gone," John said in a placatory tone of voice and, sitting down on his side of the bed, pulled on his socks and underpants and began to dress.

Breakfast, except on some days in the holidays, was always toast, cereal, orange juice, tea. The TV was on in the kitchen, only tuned to ITV. John absolutely forbade Channel 4 which he thought was full of rubbish. There were always endless arguments about the TV in the Tempest household which seemed ridiculous when one considered there was a TV set practically in every room. Each of the children had one in their bedroom, John and Helen had one in theirs. There was one in the kitchen and another in the sitting room. Yet there were always rows about what to watch on the TV.

Helen thought of the disharmony in the Becket household that Muriel had referred to. Maybe the Beckets were just ordinary people like them who quarrelled about the TV? When you were single, when you only had yourself to think of, it was easy, tempting even, to be critical of others. There was much to be said for the single life, but it could lead to selfishness; much to be said for the married state, but that had its own disadvantages too.

"I haven't seen Skittles for *ages*," Meg said, looking at the bowl of catfood by the door. "Is she about, Mum?"

"I haven't seen her for a day or two," Helen murmured, standing by the toaster.

"*Mum*—"

"Oh, she's *all right*." John impatiently looked at his watch. "Five minutes and we have to leave the house."

"But she's my cat," Meg wailed.

29

"Then you should have looked after her properly," Helen snapped, "which you haven't, since she was a kitten."

"I shall feel very *unhappy* if poor Skittles is lost . . ." Meg dug her fist in the corner of her eye.

"Of *course* she's not lost!" With an exclamation John got up.

"I'll find her by the time you get home," Helen promised looking out of the window. "It's such a nice day I promise I'll go looking for her."

Maybe she'd ask Muriel in for a coffee and suggest they take a walk.

But when the time came, the beds made and the breakfast things stacked in the dishwasher, Muriel wasn't at home. The doors of her garage were open and there was no sign of the car. On the other side of the Tempests lived a working couple, solicitors who had briefly introduced themselves and not been glimpsed since.

There were about twelve houses on the estate, each set back in its own garden, each a little different from the rest. They formed a semi-circle at the top of the hill except for Muriel's, which seemed larger than all the others and stood on its own. Apparently the developer had gone bankrupt before he had time to complete his project, which was nice for those who were there because it remained small, although there was always room for development which Muriel said she dreaded.

At about eleven Helen decided to go and look for the cat.

To start with, Helen walked slowly round the estate of eleven houses noting that most of them seemed empty, their owners away or at work. One bore signs of activity, with washing hanging on the line and the sounds of a radio or stereo from within. They all had garages and one or two had garden sheds which was a possible explanation for Skittles' disappearance. The

30

most obvious reason unless, God forbid, she had been caught by a fox or run over, was that she had been locked in somewhere.

Still, it was now almost a week. As she walked her guilt redoubled because the possibility of finding the cat alive seemed more and more remote.

It was a pleasant day, a few leaves already beginning to float gently down towards the ground and, hands in her pockets, she walked slowly at first and then more quickly as her tour of the estate finished and she followed the winding country lane to the village.

It was possible that once upon a time a farm had stood at the top of the hill and this narrow winding lane been a track leading up to it, flanked on either side by ancient hedgerows.

At the bottom of the lane a narrow bridge crossed the stream which ran through the centre of the village, meandering along by the main street, eventually joining the river further up the valley, like a peripheral artery of the bloodstream.

The village likewise was almost empty of people. It was market day in Yeovil and perhaps this was the explanation. Anyway, the few people who did pass were unknown to her. Finally at the end of the street Helen stopped outside the post office and store inspecting the array of cards that mainly offered items for sale on a notice board in the window.

After examining the mass of flowers and fresh vegetables that were arranged outside she entered the store and smiled at the woman on the other side of the counter, who gave her a friendly greeting.

"Settling in all right are you?"

"Oh I think so. The difficulty is getting used to country life. It's all so much slower than the town."

"'Spect it is." The woman, whose name Helen didn't yet know, was weighing items preparatory to packing them in a box that stood on the counter.

"You make deliveries do you?" Helen enquired with interest.

"Just locally." The woman looked critically at the dial of the scales. "Some outlying farms. We'd certainly take them up to the estate if you'd give us a ring."

"That's very kind because I haven't the use of my own car at the moment. I'm afraid though I'm here for another purpose. Our cat's disappeared and I wondered if I could put a notice in the window?"

"Oh dear, of course you can," the woman said sympathetically. "Young cat was she?"

"About three." Helen's heart lifted hopefully. "You haven't seen one or heard of anyone who has found one?"

"'Fraid not. But young cats probably take longer to settle. Did you keep her in?"

"A full week."

The woman shrugged. "Maybe that wasn't long enough."

"But we've been here nearly two months."

The shopkeeper weighed another bag of greens and frowned, more intent, obviously, on her task than the fate of the Tempest cat.

"I think she's probably been locked in somewhere." Helen paused. "I'd be very grateful if you'd ask around."

She handed the card she'd written out before leaving home to the postmistress, who glanced at it, scribbled something on the back and said, "That will be 50p for the week please."

"It seems very reasonable. Thanks." Helen gave her the coin and prepared to depart.

"Hope you get the cat back," the postmistress called kindly. "It's sad to lose a pet."

Helen went out into the street aware that the feeling of heaviness, of depression, had taken over again. She really was so volatile. Up and down these days. Now, had she been in Worcester Park she would have taken the Tube into the West End or gone to see a girl friend,

32

Pauline, if she wasn't working, or Angela. Here there was nothing to do but walk around looking for the cat, aware of her isolation, wishing in fact that she was anywhere but where she was. Tip Hollow. The end of the world.

She turned back past the post office, to the lane leading to the church, and along the village street, across the bridge and up the gradual slope of the winding lane until the houses came into view again. She noted with a sense of increasing depression that Muriel was still out and resolved that she would tackle John that very evening about the possibility of a second-hand car. It was quite ridiculous to be stranded by oneself in the country miles and miles from anywhere, deprived of human stimulus.

She stood for a moment outside Muriel's house then turned towards the garden gate which was open – she thought she'd closed it – and went slowly up the path reaching the house when the feeling of desolation seemed to overwhelm her and she stood by the door, her key poised in the latch, as if unwilling to enter.

At last she slowly, reluctantly, turned the key and opened the door. A draught of air rushed to greet her almost knocking her over as though the back door or a window had blown violently open. Once again the house seemed a cold, unfriendly place, a sad place devoid of human warmth and solace. Entering the sitting room she flung her coat on a chair and, sinking into another, leaned forward, weeping.

After a while she raised her head, aghast, hurriedly wiping her eyes. She hadn't let go like this, well, for years. But then she hadn't had this feeling of desolation, of despair, ever. Whenever she had wept in the past there had been a reason, either pain or bereavement, like when her grandmother died. Now there was none, or none that she knew of.

It was the house. She knew without any doubt that her original misgivings were right. It was an unhappy house, a house where people had fought, suffered, which had

33

forcibly been taken away from them. Now there she was – a victim, like them, of loneliness, depression and fear.

After a while Helen got up and went into the kitchen to make a cup of tea. It was nearly two and she hadn't eaten since breakfast. She was usually ravenous by lunch time. Today she'd intended to do some gardening, but then she'd set off to look for the cat. She'd meant to buy seeds at the post office as well as leave the card, but she'd forgotten. She was consumed by this free-floating sense of anxiety that seemed to have no definite, definable cause.

She filled the kettle and placed it on its base, flicked on the switch, watched it glow as the water began to boil. She opened the fridge, inspected the contents and decided she wasn't hungry. Anyway she had no bread. She had been all the way to the store and forgot to get bread, as well as seeds. She was preoccupied by the loss of the cat, this feeling of guilt.

The telephone rang and, grateful for the interruption, she ran to answer it. Maybe it was someone with news of Skittles.

"Hello?" she said putting the receiver to her ear. There was a peculiar static on the phone. Then a series of clicks. "Hello?" she said again but there was no sound. Or no sound of voices. But she felt that someone was there, listening.

She replaced the receiver and realized she was trembling. Maybe someone had stolen Skittles and . . . oh she was being absurd. She made her tea, single teabag in a mug and, sitting down again at the kitchen table, took several deep breaths. Really she was being utterly, hopelessly absurd. She was going to crack up, have a nervous breakdown. Maybe it was an early menopause? Some women had them before forty.

She remembered the pills which she had now finished. Maybe *that* was the reason. Now definitely was the time to find and register with a new doctor.

But what exactly was wrong? As Helen lifted her cup to her mouth her hand had a very slight tremor. She looked out at the sunny landscape, the tranquil, peaceful scene. Somewhere out there was Skittles, maybe trapped in a shed. The shed. Of course *they* had a shed and they had never been near it since Skittles had disappeared. Fancy not ever having thought of the shed!

Hope surged through her and she quickly finished her tea and rinsed out the cup. It would, anyway, be a very good idea to tidy out the shed. It would give her something to do.

Suddenly she felt more cheerful and, she realized, a bit peckish. She had succeeded in almost scaring herself to death. Well, she would look in the shed just to be sure. Of course reason told her that Skittles couldn't possibly be *there*; they would have heard her. Anyway the children would soon be home. Oh . . . she looked at the calendar on the wall. No they wouldn't. Today they stayed on at school for extra sports and would be collected at about six by John. She had better ring him and ask him to get some bread.

Hastily she made herself scrambled eggs, feeling heaps better now that she had thought of something practical and useful to do. She swallowed it with a fresh mug of tea and then went over to phone.

It was still dead. Well, no, it wasn't 'dead'. There was static on the line and, yes, definitely the sense of someone *there*. "Hello?" she said loudly and as the sound seemed to echo along the line she banged the receiver down, angry with herself for being so stupid. Well, she would definitely be looking round in the next few weeks for a job, for something to do. She would get a bank overdraft for the car and pay it off after she had found a job.

Feeling happier now that she had made a sensible, practical decision, Helen put on her plastic apron, donned rubber gloves and made her way to the shed at the bottom of the garden. It was secured by a wooden bolt that had cobwebs across it and looked as though it hadn't been opened for ages.

In fact, apart from glancing in it when they came to inspect the house, and ascertaining that the people before and probably the people before *them* had left all their old junk there, she didn't think anyone had been near the shed since they'd moved in. Certainly there wasn't any possibility that Skittles could be there. Still . . .

Helen stood in front of the shed aware once again of that eerie stillness that she seemed to notice so much more now that she lived in the country. There wasn't a sound; no bird song, no wind sighing in the trees. Nothing. It was uncanny, odd. She looked almost stealthily around as though fearful she herself might disturb something, someone.

She reached out and turned the bolt. A spider scurried away from the security of its hidey hole. Gently she pushed open the door and peered inside. At the end was a grimy window almost completely covered by cobwebs which allowed a little light to penetrate. A little, not much. Stacked in front of it from door to window was an assortment of sticks, old tables, garden furniture of various kinds, all in a state of advanced disrepair, plastic watering cans, tins of paint, old seed catalogues.

"Skittles," she whispered loudly, knowing quite well there would be no response.

Skittles could not possibly be there. It was only an old garden shed after all; but useful. If they could get all this stuff sorted out and taken away, John could paint it and it would be a good place to keep garden tools, the patio furniture that they intended in time to acquire.

Filled with a sudden burst of energy, laughing at her fears, she ran back to the kitchen and returned with a broom, a duster, a dustpan and brush. Then she swung the shed door open wide and began to move the assortment of debris, the bric-à-brac blocking up the entrance. She took everything outside and leaned it either against the shed or laid it on the lawn. Now she could see over the mass of jumble to the window and light finally began to penetrate so that she could see through the gloom.

The furniture was mostly cane or plastic, very light so that she could move it easily. It was incredible the amount of stuff people accumulated over the years. John could just make a pile of it all at the weekend and burn the lot. As for the paint people kept . . . years old and so congealed that none of the lids could open. She stacked the pots of paint outside the shed until finally she could see the end wall and the entire window ingrained with the dust, dirt and cobwebs of years. Maybe no one had cleaned it in the thirty years since the house was built.

Helen got on her knees and with the brush started vigorously cleaning the area of floor she'd uncovered. On one side blocking the wall was an old dresser, the only really solid piece of furniture in the shed. John and Jake could move that between them. She leaned down and reached with the brush under the dresser, but some object barred its way.

She bent right down so that her head was practically on the floor . . . and stared into the petrified face of a dead cat, its sockets eyeless, and round its neck a ligature as though it had been strangled.

Chapter Three

Muriel Forbes parked her car by the side of the house –
she would garage it later – and consulted the clock on
the dashboard.

Four o'clock. Tea time. She looked over at the Tempests' house but there was no sign of life. Not that
there ever was much activity, which she thought odd
for people who hadn't been there for very long. Of
course at weekends the children were in and out with their
bicycles, and John took them swimming at a private pool
that belonged to a nearby school most Saturday or Sunday
mornings. Otherwise there was surprisingly little toing
and froing, and not the interest in the garden she had been
led to expect from Helen, who had said that, although she
knew little about gardening, she was anxious to learn.

Why, now was the time to start preparing the ground
for the spring, and that garden could do with a good
turning over. The Beckets had had no interest in the
garden at all.

In fact now that she came to think about it there was
a similarity between the Tempests and the Beckets. The
parents were of a similar age and so were the children,
who had also been a boy and a girl. They too had a cat
which, oddly enough, had also disappeared and although
the rows that emanated from the house were considerably
louder and, she thought, more violent, she had frequently
heard sounds of discord between the Tempests, although
Helen always self-consciously laughed it off and said it
was over the television.

Yet she liked Helen Tempest, Muriel thought, opening the boot and beginning to collect the parcels she'd bought during a shopping spree in Dorchester. Half guiltily she'd wondered if she should ask Helen; but there were certain things she wanted to do, and it was so much easier to flip about by yourself than try to accommodate someone who might want to do very different things.

Yes she liked Helen and thought they could be friends eventually, though there was an age difference. She found Helen outgoing and friendly, though also rather nervous; but John . . . well she thought John was the sort of man she would never really take to. There was a wariness about him, a lack of warmth. Yes, he was definitely cold. A cold fish. As for the children, well, they had very little appeal for her. Reminded her too much of school. She had much preferred teaching sixth formers, high achievers who were going on to university.

It was a pity, in a *way*, that the house hadn't gone to an older, professional couple with whom she might have had more in common.

She was about to close the boot when the air was suddenly rent by a violent scream of such terror that her blood literally ran cold. She dropped all the parcels in her arms as, horror-struck, she looked towards the Tempest house. The scream came again, somehow even more strident and shocking, and she ran straight across the road, through the gate and up the garden path, realizing then that the scream came from round the back and not indoors. She hesitated for a moment. Even a sensible person, such as she was, dreaded what she might see, but then she ran round the back and saw Helen crouching on the floor just inside the garden shed with her head between her hands.

"My dear," she cried rushing up to her, "what's happened? Are you hurt?" She knelt on the ground, a hand on Helen's shoulder, looking for injury.

Helen didn't turn or attempt to look at her, but remained where she was crouched in a rigid position as though she had been struck by lightning. But she didn't appear to be harmed.

"Have you had a *fright*, dear?" Muriel tightened her clasp. "Whatever frightened you? Are you afraid of mice? Of spiders?"

She knelt awkwardly beside Helen trying to inspect her face, but it was still covered by her hands. Then as if aware of the comforting body next to her she leaned heavily against Muriel and lowered her hands from her face. Though her eyes remained tight shut she started to gibber something unintelligible.

"Helen dear," Muriel said in her most caring tone of voice. "Tell me, what is the matter?"

"I found the cat," she gulped. "Skittles . . . she's been strangled."

"Oh my *God*!" Muriel felt herself blanch with horror and looked around. Aware that Helen was preparing herself to scream again she gently got her to her feet and led her outside, where she made her sit down on the lawn, crouching beside her.

"Skittles, in the shed?" Muriel whispered, looking almost fearfully over her shoulder.

"Yes!" Helen violently nodded her head. "She's got something round her neck. It's just," she started shaking again, "just horrible. I've had such an awful day. I *knew* something bad was going to happen. I felt so uneasy, so tense, so worried about the cat." She gazed reproachfully at Muriel. "I looked for you . . ."

Muriel started guiltily. If only she'd *asked* her.

"I had to go to Dorchester on business. I had to see my accountant . . ."

But why make all the excuses? After all she had a right to do exactly what she liked with her time.

"I thought Skittles *might* be in the shed," Helen went on, tears beginning to flow freely down her face. "It

40

suddenly occurred to me. But there were cobwebs on the latch and I thought it hadn't been opened for months. So I decided to tidy it out and thought John and Jake could make a bonfire at the weekend."

"Tell me where the cat is," Muriel said, not relishing her task.

"Under the dresser. She's still there."

"But who could . . . how?"

"I don't know." Helen started to shake again. "It's all so horrible . . ."

Muriel had no real inclination to look in the shed herself. After all, some things were unpleasant even for such a sensible, unemotional person as she thought herself to be; no, *knew* herself to be.

However it had to be done and leaving Helen on the lawn she went into the shed, got down on her knees and peered under the dresser.

It was certainly not a very attractive sight; but one thing struck her immediately.

"This animal has been dead for years," she called over her shoulder. "The atmosphere in the shed must have petrified it. The Beckets lost a cat. It's probably theirs."

"Oh *no!*" Helen got shakily to her feet. "It's *not* Skittles?"

"No chance." Feeling braver now, Muriel looked around for an object with which to poke the carcass out. She seized the hoe leaning against the wall and stuck it under the dresser.

Then very gradually she drew out the cat's body, so that it lay on the floor between her and the door.

It was sad, it was pathetic to think the creature must have got stuck. Died of starvation, a lingering death. Something else struck her.

"You can see it wasn't strangled," she cried, her voice ringing with relief. "That's its *collar.*"

"Oh, the collar!" Helen exclaimed.

"Your cat didn't wear a collar did she?"

41

"No."

"It's much much too old for her anyway. Poor thing." Muriel stirred it with the hoe. "I can see why it gave you such a fright though. Look, if you can get me one of those black bags I'll get rid of it for you."

"You're so kind," Helen said, her voice beginning to sound more assured, normal.

"It would give anyone a shock," Muriel said stoutly. "Especially someone a bit nervy, worried about the cat."

"I was never nervy before I came here," Helen said indignantly and then, unexpectedly, again burst into tears.

Muriel finally got Helen back to the kitchen and sat her down while she made a pot of strong tea.

"Fancy a brandy?" she asked as she placed the cup in front of her neighbour who shook her head.

"I'll be OK. It was just a shock."

"Well of course it was horrible. But you must have known it *couldn't* be Skittles."

"I just didn't think logically." Helen raised the cup to her lips and drank deeply. Slowly the colour was returning to her cheeks. "I've been kind of strung up all day. I woke up with a headache. I began to worry seriously about the cat. I wished," she looked anxiously across the table, "I *wished* you were there, and I could have had someone to talk to."

Once again Muriel felt a pang of guilt. It would have been so easy to have taken her to Dorchester and then none of this would have happened. On the other hand it might have happened some time when Helen or someone else was alone. Someone had to clear out that shed and the cat would have been found. It might have been one of the children, Meg for instance, in which case the damage might have been worse. But if it had been the prosaic John, he would just

42

have chucked it aside and thought nothing more of it.

"Really I thought it *was* Skittles." Helen shook again. "That fur. Horrible."

"Well, of course, it doesn't decay like flesh—"

"Please," Helen held up a hand. "Anyway I thought Skittles might have been shut in somewhere. I had it on my mind. You know how cats are. I looked all round the estate up here and then I went to the village and put a notice in the post office window."

"Of course you had the cat on your mind all day . . ." Muriel smiled sympathetically and then lifted her head as she heard the phone ring.

"Shall I answer it?"

"Would you mind? I still feel a bit shaky."

Muriel nodded and went off to answer the phone while Helen helped herself to more tea. She was feeling better but she definitely would see the doctor and get some more pills. Her nerves were all on edge.

Muriel came back into the kitchen shaking her head. "Wrong number I guess."

Helen looked up sharply. "Did anyone speak to you?"

"No. They just seemed to listen and then hang up."

"That happened to me this morning. I felt someone was there. Listening."

"Oh, no, I didn't feel that." Muriel emphatically shook her head and then, pouring herself fresh tea, sat opposite Helen.

"You know your nerves *are* in a pretty bad way aren't they? Were you always, a," – she hesitated – "a bit on the nervous side?"

"Not at all," Helen said robustly. "Not in the slightest." She ran a hand over her face. "It seems that since we decided to move . . . or rather *I* didn't want to move, you see. I was happy where I was."

"So you said; but in marriage – I mean I've never been married – but doesn't one have to sort of fit

43

in with the partner? Being single makes you terribly selfish."

"I just felt John didn't think about *me* or the children. Moving them at that age was a terrible risk. As it is they're both quite bright and they've settled in well. They're clever and well adjusted and that helps. In fact I think if anything this school is better than the last. Then, of course, it was a great step up for John to have his own branch. It was promotion, also more money."

"Well then . . ." Muriel attempted a practical smile.

"But what about *me*? I have a right to a life too."

"Of course you have."

"I had all my friends in Worcester Park." Helen's voice became querulous. "I had a part-time job in which I was very happy. I could go to the West End whenever I felt like a shopping spree or a day out. Now I'm dumped in the heart of the countryside, a place I never saw in my life before, where I know no one and . . ." Close to tears again, she stopped. "Do you think I'm getting the menopause?" she asked, her voice suddenly child-like and pathetic.

Muriel looked nonplussed.

"How old are you?"

"Thirty-five."

"Isn't that a bit early for the menopause?"

"They say you can get it early."

"Oh you *can*. But most people don't. I mean have you seen the doctor?"

"I saw my doctor at home . . . in Worcester Park. He gave me a sedative and an anti-depressant."

"Oh, then you *did* have trouble there?"

"It only started *after* John got offered the job and we came down here and he set his heart on a house like *this*, in the middle of nowhere, just because it had been repossessed and was cheap." Helen, her voice impassioned, brought her fist down on the table. "*That's* really what makes me so angry."

*   *   *

John Tempest sat outside the school drumming his fingers on the wheel of the car. He felt vaguely gloomy, dissatisfied with life. The job was not what he thought it would be. He realized he had liked all the travel associated with selling insurance, and now he found himself stuck behind a desk for most of the day dealing with difficult customers or sorting out problems connected with his staff; many of them were trainees and completely new to the business.

John lit a cigarette and tucked the match neatly into the ashtray. In fact he wasn't very good with people and maybe he should have thought of that when he accepted a job which would involve managing a lot of staff. He'd only ever had to deal with his colleagues and secretaries, and clients were a different matter because however difficult they might be one was never with them for long.

And then there was this place. *Really* provincial, and both he and Helen were suburban types. He hadn't considered that. The last thing he would do would be to admit it to her, but it was true. And how stupid it had been to buy a house in a place like Tip Hollow – so remote, miles from anywhere. Besides, with the exception of Muriel, the neighbours were unfriendly, typical of ex-city dwellers – like themselves.

Well, he was reluctant to admit it, but the motivation had been greed. He couldn't resist a bargain like that, thirty thousand off the anticipated price. Well, maybe they'd sell it soon and move nearer the town. Not that much went on in Yeovil after five in the afternoon, when all the shops closed and the place seemed to shut down for the night. Not like London, when the shops kept open and the lights went on shining.

He looked at the illuminated clock on the dashboard. It was getting dark. Soon the clocks would go back and they would be into winter. Real winter with dark afternoons,

45

frosty nights and maybe snow. Perhaps they'd be snowed up. God forbid. He shivered.

There was a stirring outside the school building and suddenly two faces looked at him through the window. Cheerful, smiling faces. Thank heaven for that.

"Jump in," he said leaning over to open the passenger door. "Had a good day?"

"Fine! Fine," they chorused. Meg jumped in next to her father, and Jake sat in the back after putting their kit in the boot of the car. John turned to look at them in the gloom, appreciating their happy expressions, their lithe, animal-like young bodies exuberant with good spirits, teeming with health.

"It will soon be dark," he said putting the car into gear after inspecting the rear mirror.

"We can play basketball indoors," Meg said.

"I can do some homework after football," Jake volunteered. "Will you go on picking us up at this time, Daddy?"

"I expect so." John drove out of the town and, half-way up the hill outside Yeovil, he made a sharp turn to the right and drove up a narrow lane with overhanging trees that formed a long dark arch. In summertime it was very pretty. In winter, with the shadows made by the lights of the car dancing about, it was rather sinister.

John remained largely silent during the drive while the children chattered to each other animatedly about the events of the day. What a relief it was, what a help to have happy, healthy, *normal* children who hadn't been the least as uprooted as their parents had half expected them to be. They even seemed to welcome the change of schools, to enjoy it, and quickly made new friends.

When the car stopped outside the door it was quite dark, but lights glowed from within the house and above the garage, whose door was open.

John decided that he would leave his anxieties and worries about the day firmly behind and after the children

46

had got out, drove the car straight into the garage, removed his briefcase and a couple of packages and closed the main garage door, exiting by the side door that went directly into the kitchen. There to his surprise he found their neighbour Muriel Forbes standing by the stove stirring a pot that stood on top of it.

John and the children entered the kitchen simultaneously and stood looking at her from the doors at opposite ends.

"My goodness is it as late as that already?" Guiltily, Muriel glanced at the clock on the wall and, after a final sniff, put the lid back on the pot.

"Where's Helen?" John asked abruptly, momentarily aware of a feeling of panic. "Is she all right?"

"She's got a headache and is lying down," Muriel said. "I offered to pop in and organize dinner."

"That's very kind of you." John put his things down and, removing his jacket, draped it over the back of one of the kitchen chairs.

"No trouble at all."

"It got worse? She had one this morning."

"Yes. It wasn't a very pleasant day." Muriel looked over her shoulder at Meg, who stood staring solemnly at her. "She's all right, really."

"Can we go up and see?"

"Well I think she's asleep." Muriel came over to the kitchen table and sat down, looking rather tired herself. "Actually she did have a bit of a shock." She put out her hand to quell their anxiety. "But she *is* all right. I promise you that."

John lit a cigarette and leaned against the kitchen dresser.

"What kind of shock?"

"Well," Muriel seemed to be steeling herself for the tale, "you know she was very worried about the cat—"

"Oh, nothing's *happened* to Skittles . . ." Meg began with a wail, but Muriel smiled at her reassuringly.

47

"No. We haven't found her, but no news is good news isn't it? Anyway your mother had the fate of the cat on her mind and, well, not *feeling* very well herself, she went down to the village to put a notice in the post office window. When she came back she felt a little better so she decided, rather foolishly you may think, to clear out the garden shed."

"The garden *shed!*" Jake gasped. "But we haven't been in there since we came. Dad says it's full of rubbish. I was going to do it for Scouts' 'bob a job' week."

"And so it is. Your mother had an idea the cat may *somehow* have managed to get inside which, of course, it hadn't, but while she was moving the furniture," Muriel paused and took a deep breath, "she did, very unfortunately, find a mummified cat which must have got stuck inside a long time ago and well . . . it was dead of course."

"Oh how *awful!*" Meg put her face in her hands, a gesture which reminded Muriel of her mother. In fact mother and daughter were very alike: short, slightly plumpish, but attractive with curly brown hair.

"Yes, your mother had a terrible shock and . . . well, it was the same colour as your cat. Fur doesn't putrefy like flesh and naturally she thought the worst. I heard her cry, luckily I had just got in, and went over. I was able immediately to reassure her that it had been dead for ages, and we had a cup of tea and she calmed down. Then the headache started to come on badly. Does she get migraine?" Muriel looked curiously up at John, who shook his head.

"She hardly ever gets headaches."

"Well today she did and it was just too bad." She went back over to the stove and lifted the lid of the pot. "Look, there's a casserole in here. Helen had it ready and all I had to do was heat it up. The vegetables are cooked and in the oven and if you don't mind I'd better get back to my own home."

48

"It's very, very kind of you," John said again as if returning from a reverie. "Are you sure you won't eat with us?"

"No thanks, really. I've got some work to do."

"Work? You work?"

"Well I do a lot of work, voluntary, part-time, you know the kind of thing, societies and such like. When you retire, believe me, you seem to find far more things to do than you ever had before."

"A glass of sherry?"

"I won't, thank you, really." Now that they were at home Muriel seemed anxious to be gone. She flung a cardigan over her shoulder and prepared to leave by the back door.

John accompanied her round the house and, as they were about to go along the path, he stopped and said, "What happened to the cat?"

"The cat?"

"The corpse."

"Oh!" Muriel's hand flew to her mouth. "I meant to put it in a bag, but I forgot. I'm afraid it's still there."

"I'd better move it," John said.

"Yes." Muriel paused and looked at him. "It's really not a very pretty sight. Shall I come with you?"

"Oh no, there's no need."

"Don't be so *brave*." Muriel gave him a friendly little tap on the arm. "Besides it all happened so quickly I want to be sure I didn't leave anything there. You'd better get a torch," she said, looking past him, "it's pitch-dark, and for heaven's sake *don't* tell the children what you're going to do."

It was indeed very dark and she walked slowly towards the shed, rather regretting her impulsive offer. After all he was a man, not a very sensitive one, she thought, and she was sure he would be quite able to deal with the mummified corpse of a dead cat. Outlined in the gloom the shed seemed strangely sinister. She felt a flicker of unease, of apprehension, and wished she were back in the warmth and comfort of her own home.

Really, having neighbours like the Tempest didn't do one's nerves any good. And the Beckets had been no better. It really was like bad luck to have two turbulent, unsettling families as her neighbours.

John was soon back, shining the beam of the torch along the path. Muriel had put the door to, and she thought he hesitated rather a long time before he took hold of the handle and pulled it open. Maybe not as brave as he seemed.

The beam shone immediately on to the cat left lying on the floor and John gave a sharp intake of breath.

"I warned you it was rather horrible," Muriel said. "I should have put it in a sack while it was still light."

"It is *very* like Skittles." John bent to examine it more closely.

"The Beckets also lost a puss, and I think this is it. You can see it's been dead ages."

"Oh, sure I can, sure. What's that round its neck?" He peered more closely. "It looks as though it's been strangled."

"That's what Helen said." Muriel managed to laugh. "It's its *collar*."

"Oh, of course." John's laughter was apologetic. "Works wonders on the imagination this time of night doesn't it?"

"I'm afraid so."

"Skittles didn't have a collar."

"It's not her anyway . . ."

"Of course not." John still seemed nonplussed by the appearance of the cat and looked round as if he wasn't quite sure what to do.

"Why don't you get a spade while I go back and get a bin liner?" Muriel suggested. "I should have done it this afternoon."

"Good idea." John shone the torch on the range of

50

garden implements leaning against the wall and then, selecting a rusty spade, waited for Muriel, who soon appeared shaking out a large black bag.

"There, pop it in," she said briskly. "And for heaven's sake let's forget all about it."

She found, however, that it was easier said than done, and after she got back to the warmth of her own home the spectacle lingered in the mind and she helped herself to a large measure of whisky.

Helen lay staring up at the shadows on the ceiling. It was hard to believe that so much had happened in the past twenty-four hours. It was only this time last night that she'd been thinking over the events of the past week, trying to remember exactly when it was that Skittles had disappeared. She was a cat who always had tended to come and go, though in Worcester Park she never exactly went missing, never stayed away for days. She usually spent the day indoors and the nights prowling around, like most cats. It was only because she, Helen, had been so busy that they hadn't realized no one had actually seen the cat for some days.

But why should Skittles disappear? She was a domestic cat, a loved and loving cat, well looked after, well fed. Had something in the house upset her? With her strange feline intuition had she divined something that Helen had instinctively realized all along?

Something about the house wasn't quite right. It was no use pretending now. It was *not* a happy house, and they were not happy here. She was having strange fits of anxiety and depression and John was sleeping badly. He was tossing about now and she doubted whether he was asleep. That day she had had the most ghastly headache, one of the worst she had ever had, and she didn't have many. She had been ill at ease all day, lonely and restless, and then there'd been that horrible episode

51

with the corpse of the cat. She would be haunted by it for the rest of her life.

"Are you awake?" John said softly beside her.

"Yes."

"I thought you were. How's the head?"

"Better."

"Good."

"It was the most *awful* headache."

"Muriel said so. She's very good. Made our dinner."

"She was *very* good to me today. Calm and practical. I nearly went out of my mind when I found—"

"I know, I saw it." John's arm slid round her. "It upset me too."

"*What*, you went and had a look?" Helen turned her head towards him.

"Yes. I didn't want the children to find it, or you to see it again."

"That was very kind of you." Helen, touched, paused. "Very brave too."

"Muriel came with me."

"Oh she did." Helen gave a brief laugh. "What did you do with it?"

"Put it in a bag and threw it away. Forget about it."

"I don't think I ever shall."

"You must. We must settle down here Helen."

"Why do you say that?"

"Because we must. For the time being. Maybe we'll move to Yeovil in a couple of years."

"A *couple* of years!"

"Well we can't move now. We've just arrived."

"I feel we've been here forever."

"You really aren't happy here are you?"

"No."

"I'm not either."

"I know."

"It's nothing to do with the house. I mean, I quite *like* the house and the place. I'm not sure I'm the right man

52

for the job I've got. You know I liked being on the road selling things, moving about. I'm stuck all day in the office dealing with problems and people."

"Do you think you made a mistake?"

"I don't know. I thought at the time it was right. I thought very hard about it."

"But you didn't think about *me*. Didn't take me into account."

"No, maybe I didn't think hard enough."

"No 'maybe' about it. You didn't think at *all*."

"Is that why you're not happy? Really? It's not the place or the house?"

"I am bored out of my mind, John. I am not a country woman. I don't really *like* the country. I mean I think it's pretty and everything, but I'm not sure I'm cut out to live here. And no, I definitely don't like this house. I never did. It's an unhappy house, I know that for sure now."

"Don't be silly," John said loosening his grip on her shoulders and pecking her on the cheek. "Houses can't be unhappy. They're bricks and mortar. I've never believed in ghosts. It's people, living people, who are unhappy. But I believe our fate is in our hands, we are in control. And really we must do all we can for the next two years, at least, to make the best of what we've got. I mean we have to." He moved away from her, lying on his side after checking the time. "We can't ever go back to Worcester Park."

"Why not?"

He felt the despair in her voice and it shocked him. He reached for her hand under the bedclothes and pressed it.

"You know why not. We'd look like fools. Everyone would laugh at us. You never know," he said in a different tone of voice, "something might turn up."

"What sort of thing?" She sounded surprised.

He twisted restlessly in bed.

"You never know. A windfall. Life's full of surprises."

"You don't even do the pools," she said derisively.
"You never know. Trust me." He gave a deep sigh.
"Anyway I'd never get my old job back. You can't turn
back the clock you know, Helen, you can't."

Yet wasn't that exactly what was happening now she
thought, aggrieved, as his breathing grew regular and his
body began to relax beside her. The clock was turning
right back, to whoever or whatever haunted the house.

Chapter Four

Helen had dressed with unusual care, taking time to select the right outfit, apply make-up and fix her hair in a manner she judged would give a good impression: neither too young nor too old; mutton, for instance, dressed up as lamb. Brisk, capable, calm . . . well not exactly *calm* perhaps at the moment, inwardly anyway, but for a few crucial hours she thought she could manage it.

After all she was only trying to be herself; her old self, her true self. The sort of person she had been before she came to Tip Hollow. Yes, she was normally a brisk, calm and capable person, fully up to the part-time job she'd enjoyed in Worcester Park.

Now she sat opposite her interviewer at the employment agency, in a bright sun-filled room over the Quedam shopping precinct in Yeovil from the window of which was a nice view of the church.

The interviewer, Mrs Maddox, was about the same age as she, also suitably dressed to present an image of calm, capability. Two of a kind it would seem, yet, idly, Helen wondered what went on in *her* private life.

Mrs Maddox smiled at her and then looked at the papers on her desk; the result of the tests she'd given Helen over the past hour; her shorthand speed, word processing skills and a range of simple psychological and aptitude tests. Helen felt she'd acquitted herself rather well and sat there feeling self-confident, calmly watching Mrs Maddox's reaction.

"Well," finally Mrs Maddox looked up and joined

her hands together, "clearly you're very capable, Mrs Tempest. You worked for how long at the builders?"

"Just over five years." Helen felt a flicker of pride at the implication she'd combined work with bringing up a family.

"And you left?" Mrs Maddox scribbled something in the margin of one of the papers.

"Well shortly after we decided to come here. I mean my husband accepted the job . . . about" – Helen shrugged – "six months ago."

"Six months." Mrs Maddox duly noted the facts on the sheet of paper. Then she put down her pencil and her level gaze met Helen.

"As I said, you're clearly very capable, Mrs Tempest, but, frankly, your skills are not *quite* up to what would be expected in a modern office here. You made rather too many typing mistakes." Quickly her eyes ran down a list. "You weren't entirely familiar with the WP."

"That's a model I hadn't used," Helen said defensively.

"Understandable," Mrs Maddox nodded pleasantly, "and allowances *have* been made. But these days one has to be instantly adaptable and younger women *are*. They learn things more quickly you see and to be perfectly honest," she flashed her a sympathetic smile, "they are more in demand."

"I don't see why."

"Neither do I. I mean most of them run off and get married within a year or two, and whatever they say few of them stay on after they've had a baby. Times haven't really changed all that much have they?" Her expression became conspiratorial, as though one woman of the world confiding in another.

Helen swallowed hard. "Do I understand, then, that after all this time, all these tests, you have no position for me?"

"Not at the *moment* Mrs Tempest." Mrs Maddox

carefully emphasized the word 'moment'. "That is not to say that *if* a vacancy should occur where someone of your qualifications and abilities seems suitable, of course I should notify you immediately. Some employers occasionally do ask for older women, but," once more she flashed that bright and, Helen now decided, rather insincere smile, "not often. They like young women, with one or two O levels as well as first-class secretarial skills. Have you got a word processor by the way?"

"No."

Mrs Maddox scribbled herself another note.

"If I were you it might be a good idea to acquire one and practise." She stood up. "Practise makes perfect you know."

Helen, however, stubbornly remained where she was.

"There's absolutely nothing? A receptionist?"

Mrs Maddox gave a tinkly laugh.

"*All* receptionists these days have to work jolly hard. They don't just sit there with smiles on their faces. They have to work the switchboard *and* type." Mrs Maddox perched on the edge of the desk. "If you're really *that* desperate, Mrs Tempest, and I can see that you may be, tell me have you ever thought of domestic work?"

"Domestic work?" Helen blinked.

"Have you ever thought, for instance, of working as a cleaner? Industrial cleaners are very well paid. Or work in a school." She got up from her desk and punched in the keys of the VDU, scanning the screen. "We've nothing at the moment because so many local authorities are going private, but just for that reason dinner ladies are often needed at short notice."

"I'll bear that in mind," Helen said with an attempt at a dignity she didn't feel and, standing up, she smoothed down the carefully chosen skirt. A *dinner* lady, indeed.

"I realize it's not the sort of thing you're after. But if you want to get out of the house . . . would

57

you like me to give you a call if something turns up?"

"I'll have to talk to my husband," Helen said circumspectly. "See what he thinks."

"What a good idea." Mrs Maddox seemed relieved that the buck had been passed further along the line and looked at the clock on the wall. "Now, if you'll excuse me." She opened the door and led the way through reception. "I'm *so* sorry. I really am; but these are hard times you know. People say the recession is over, but I don't think it is. Not by a long chalk."

Helen guiltily paid off the taxi and hurried up the path. Seven pounds! John would have a fit if he knew. Well he wouldn't, because she certainly wouldn't tell him. She'd intended to spend the day in Yeovil shopping, having lunch, maybe, to celebrate a new job. Instead she'd been turned down. Firmly and ignominiously turned down. Skills not good enough. Too old.

In the circumstances the last thing she wanted was to hang around and spend money. Money anyway that she'd now spent on a taxi. Besides, that funny headache was coming on again, accompanied by the by now all too familiar sense of dread. Fear of the unknown. She really should get the name of the nearest doctor from Muriel and go on another course of pills.

Her neighbour in the house next door was emerging from the garage having just parked her car. Or maybe she was going out. Helen didn't know and didn't care. They were a couple who worked and she doubted if she would have recognized them if she'd met them in the street. Their faces were fuzzy, not unfriendly, but impersonal blobs across the garden fence. She waved vaguely as she stood in the porch before looking for the key in her handbag, but her wave wasn't returned. Maybe the woman hadn't noticed her.

She felt rejected, isolated, alone and unwanted. She

fumbled with the key in the door latch trying hard to fight against the jumble of emotions that threatened all at once to overwhelm her.

As she opened the door the telephone rang and flinging aside her bag she rushed to answer it. Maybe Mrs Maddox had second thoughts.

"Hello?" she cried.

The line seemed to echo "hello". But it was her own voice. She could imagine the telephone line as a way of telepathic communication from one unknown force to another.

Maybe the house *was* possessed. Possessed by an alien influence that communicated by means of the telephone. Possession and repossession. She shivered at the *double entendre*, fact blending with fiction.

Her hand shook as she replaced the receiver and she went into the kitchen to make a cup of tea. She had had no lunch but she didn't want any. A day that had been full of promise at the beginning had turned once more to disaster.

It was now November and by three o'clock it was nearly dark. She gazed out of the window, at the skeletal trees, across at the shed. That horrible shed which she hadn't re-entered since she'd found the corpse of the cat. She hardly ever thought of Skittles now. Poor Skittles. Someone suggested she'd made her way back to London trying to find her former home. One read about cats doing that sort of thing and taking months, or years, in the process.

She drank her tea, still in the clothes she'd worn to her interview. Her best clothes; chosen with care.

Cleaner indeed. Dinner lady. And after all that she'd forgotten to go to the supermarket and get some provisions. She didn't in the least feel like climbing the hill in the dark, laden with goods so she made a list of the things she wanted and went to the phone to ring John.

The line was dead. No not dead. Living. There was

definitely something alive at the other end of the phone. She ran out of the kitchen, flung open the front door and saw a light in Muriel's house.

She banged so furiously on Muriel's door that Muriel looked quite startled when she opened it.

"Helen? Is everything all right?"

"It's that blasted phone," Helen cried. "There's something *wrong* with it. May I report it out of order?"

"Of course." Muriel stood back and looked at her with concern. "How did the interview go?"

"Oh don't talk to me about *that*."

"Oh! It was like that was it? Have you had a cup of tea?"

"Yes thanks. I wanted John to get some things from Tesco. I forgot."

"Well if there's anything you need . . ." She thought for a moment. "Look why don't you go back to the house and I'll try to ring you. And if there's no reply I'll report it out of order and you can ring John from here."

"I tell you it *is* out of order," Helen insisted. "It rang and I picked it up and there was no one there. Then I wanted to ring and I got the same hollow sound . . . rather like an echo."

"Look," Muriel said in an exaggeratedly patient tone of voice, "*I'll* go to the house and you ring *me* from here."

Helen stared at her aggressively.

"Why should it be any different for you?"

"Well just to see."

"You think I'm making it up, don't you?"

"Of course I don't." Muriel momentarily put a hand on her arm. Then she moved towards the door. "Now just give me a couple of minutes and then ring." She opened the door and looked out. "I see you've left your door open. I shan't be a tick." And Helen, feeling slighted, offended, as if she knew Muriel thought she wasn't all there, gazed after her.

Muriel waved cheerily from her doorway and disappeared inside. Helen counted ten and then tapped in her number. Immediately there was a ringing sound and a few seconds later the bright voice of Muriel. "Helen?"

"Yes."

"It's perfectly OK."

"Now *you* ring me," Helen insisted stubbornly and the same process was repeated with, as she knew would happen, the phone ringing and Muriel's schoolmistressy voice at the other end.

"OK," she said and replaced the receiver.

Muriel came slowly back into the house and found Helen standing by the phone as she'd left her.

"I can't understand it," Helen said, shaking her head wearily. "I just don't *know* what's the matter."

"Let's have a sherry," Muriel suggested again, putting the comforting hand once more on her arm.

"But it's only four o'clock."

"You can drink sherry any time." Muriel's manner was reassuring, supportive. "Or would you prefer a brandy?"

Helen snatched her arm away.

"There's nothing wrong with *me* you know, Muriel. I'm not mad."

"Oh I know you're not. Don't be silly."

"There's some sort of intermittent fault on the telephone."

"They're always the worst those intermittent faults," Muriel agreed immediately. "Make you feel really silly. I once had a TV that kept going wrong and every time I sent for the repair man it was perfectly OK. I think he thought I fancied him!"

Muriel stood by the sideboard in her nicely, but rather impersonally, furnished sitting room and poured two glasses of sherry. She turned and handed one to Helen, who had slumped into a chair. Muriel's house always made her feel that theirs was rather shabby. Maybe

61

they should have bought all new furniture when they bought a new house, but John was always too careful with money. In a new house, though, the old furniture did look shabby.

"I gather the interview didn't go too well." Muriel sat opposite Helen, leaning forward, anxious to help, her glass in her hand. Muriel was always so exact, so in control. One could never imagine her getting in the sort of state Helen so frequently found herself in these days. Also she was probably much nearer the menopause than Helen, if not actually over it. Helen took a sip from her glass.

"She said I was not properly qualified and too old anyway."

"What rubbish."

"That's what *I* thought at first. But by the end she had convinced me. Actually I thought I did quite well. My shorthand is eighty-seven words a minute, which is a good average, and I thought I acquitted myself quite well with the word processor, which was a model I'd never used anyway. Then she said there's a job shortage in Yeovil."

"That's true." Muriel sipped her sherry. "In the whole of the south west to be precise."

"I would have thought there was *something*. Something part-time. She asked me if I'd mind domestic work."

"Domestic work?" Muriel looked puzzled.

"Work as a cleaner. Or a dinner lady."

Muriel shifted her glass from one hand to the other, crossed and uncrossed her legs, clearly ill at ease.

"Not quite your style, I'd have thought."

"I'm not a snob."

"Of course not."

"I said I'd talk it over with my husband. But I haven't the slightest intention of doing it."

"Then what are you going to do?"

"Well stay put I suppose. For the time being."

Muriel knew she should try to involve Helen in some

of her activities. But somehow she didn't want to. She liked Helen, but she wasn't a soul mate. For one thing she was much younger. Also Muriel had made a life for herself out of her single state which she found satisfying. She had made the best of it and, in fact, her lifestyle was envied by many of her married friends.

The only blip in a well-ordered career was to have to take early retirement. But now this forced inactivity had been turned to good use. After a lifetime of work and putting something by she had plenty of money. She owned her house, a nice car, and now she was enjoying herself by participating in a number of activities, interests, which she knew Helen didn't share. Why should she, therefore, feel guilty?

Why indeed?

Muriel refilled their glasses even though Helen said she really must be going.

"You haven't told John yet about the interview I suppose?"

"Of course not. I couldn't get through."

"Oh I forgot. You were going to ring him from here."

"So I was." Helen smiled and got up smoothing her skirt. "That sherry was a good idea. You must think I'm a neurotic fool, Muriel."

"Whatever gave you that idea?" Muriel also rose and put her glass on the table by the side of her chair. "I quite agree with you about intermittent faults, and anyone would be annoyed to be told at their age that they were too old for a job. Thirty-five, I ask you!"

"It's the trend. John thought he had to accept his because when he was over forty he wouldn't be offered another. They put you out to grass early these days. I just think," Helen ran her finger along the surface of the highly polished table, "I just think our real mistake was to come here. To Tip Hollow. We should have lived in the town, in Yeovil itself. Without transport it's just ghastly living here, and John doesn't realize it. It was a real shock and I was not prepared for it." Helen went to the door and turned. "Thanks for the sherry."

"But you were going to ring John?"

Helen vaguely fluttered a hand. "Oh it's too late now. He won't be pleased if he's just about to leave work. I can manage until tomorrow. Oh by the way," Helen paused and looked momentarily embarrassed, "I think we really should register with a doctor. You know . . ."

"Oh, of course you must. We don't have a doctor in this village but I can recommend the practice in the next village. I'll give you the telephone number tomorrow."

"Thanks again for everything, Muriel."

"Any time," Muriel said with a cheery smile. All the same she stood by the window watching Helen as she made her way back to the house, her smile quickly fading.

She saw an unhappy woman. A woman in trouble.

John, of course, thought it was nonsense that she was too old for a job, or not properly qualified. He would, he said, have been quite happy to employ a woman of her age and with her skills. Of course it was out of the question that he should employ her, but he thought it was just a question of time until she found something.

"I knew you'd say that."

"Why did you know I'd say that?"

"Because you don't really care if I get a job or not."

"Frankly," he looked round, "I think there's plenty to do here. You haven't even started on the garden, and the house—"

"Yes?" She looked up sharply from loading the dishwasher, instantly alert for criticism, but John didn't reply and continued to clear the table.

As usual John was helping her after supper while the children did their homework in their bedrooms. They were very disciplined that way. Besides, now the nights were dark there was no urge to go out and play. They played very well together, which was just as well as there were no other children of their ages on the estate. Of course there were in the village, some of whom went to the same school, but Helen and John objected to the long walk down the lonely lane in the dark so, for the winter at least, such activity was out.

Jake, however, had his computer games and Meg was a great reader. They were easily manageable, likeable children. Their utter adaptability and normality sometimes made Helen feel rather foolish. *She* was the one who made all the fuss whereas they too had left behind all their friends, a familiar way of life as well. On the other hand they had each other. She only had a neighbour twenty years her senior with whom she felt little in common.

John finished putting everything neatly in the cupboards and shook the tablecloth out of the back door.

"You were saying," Helen prompted him as he came in and shut the door.

"Was I?"

"About the house."

"Well. It *is* getting terribly untidy. I mean not like it used to be, and that was when you had a job. You don't seem to notice it. I think you spend too much time sitting around brooding, Helen. This thing about the telephone is ridiculous. Look," John took it off the hook, listened to the dialling tone and held it out to her, "no one there."

"I *know* there's no one there."

"Listen for yourself," he urged, shaking the receiver in front of her face in a rather unpleasant, aggressive manner.

"No thank *you*." She angrily shook her head and, finishing stacking the machine, put soap powder into the container, closed it and turned it on.

"It's perfectly all right," he insisted.

"I *know* it is."

"Then why do you say there's something wrong?"

"Because there is. It's an intermittent fault."

"But you told me you thought there was someone *there.*"

"Well I did." Helen straightened up twisting back a piece of hair which had fallen over her face. "It was a queer feeling. It's all very well while you're here and the children. But when I'm alone—"

"You'll just have to face up to it, Helen. You'll just have to put up with it. Why can't you find some friends? Go out more with Muriel."

"Because Muriel has her own life. Besides she's twenty years older than I am. She's hardly like Pauline, or Angela or—"

"Why don't you invite them down?" John put the tea cloth neatly back on its rail. He was always so neat about everything. So meticulous.

"What, here?"

"Pauline would love it."

"What about Sharon?" Sharon was Pauline's daughter who had been a friend of Meg's. "She can't come in the middle of term."

"Maybe someone could look after Sharon. Or, look, why not wait until Christmas? It's not so far off, then they can both come. Or Angela—"

"She never leaves her husband."

"Well we don't want *him,*" John said grumpily. He was an Inspector of Police and seemingly omniscient. He and John had nothing in common at all.

"John I simply *must* have a car." Helen flopped down on one of the kitchen chairs and stared earnestly up at him. "It would be completely different if I was independent. My life would change and I wouldn't get so depressed, let my imagination get on top of me. I know I imagine things about the phone. About the place." She looked fearfully around. "At times I still feel it's creepy. I shall never ever be happy here I know; but if I had a car it would make it at least endurable until we can afford to move."

"That won't be for a few years," John snapped. "And as for a car it is quite out of the question—"

"But you can get them very *cheaply* in the country—"

"And think of the endless expense on maintenance and repairs. Then there's the road licence, the insurance. You're looking at a couple of thousand pounds and *that's* just for starters. Frankly we can't afford it." He stopped and looked bewilderedly at her for a few moments. "You've always been such a *sensible* person, Helen. Frankly I can't understand you."

She didn't understand him either, Helen thought the following morning as she stood doing the ironing in front of the television set. It was a cold, dark, grey morning and she'd seen John and the children off with hardly a word. She and her husband had kept very firmly to their own sides of the bed during the night as though to emphasize the gap between them; the deepening chasm in their lives.

It was all very well for John to go trundling off in the car with the children, bubbling and laughing even in weather like this and looking forward to the day. John would have meetings, talks, discussions. He might have a business lunch in a local pub. All day long the children were talking, learning, playing, communicating. She banged the iron down and looked at the ceiling. What sort of communication, for God's sake, did she have here except the inane chatter of the morning TV programmes where everyone seemed glamorous, rich and fulfilled?

Soon after John left she'd seen Muriel also leave, flapping her arm out of the window in a vague sort of wave as she sped off down the hill almost as though she were saying at the same time, "I'm free and you aren't. You're a prisoner in your own home." Of course Muriel would say nothing of the kind, but that seemed to Helen, looking for ways to be easily offended, the implication.

Worcester Park was never what you'd call a romantic

67

place, not even remotely pretty but, goodness, it was paradise compared to Tip Hollow. She finished the shirt she was ironing (John always liked drip-dry shirts to be carefully pressed) and, after folding it carefully, she put it on the table near the window on top of a pile of other shirts, sheets, table linen, her own blouses. People very seldom ironed anything these days but once she started on John's things she always thought she might as well do the rest.

Well there was really, truth to tell, scarcely anything else to do.

She gazed morosely out of the window at the misty landscape, the heavy boughs of the rain-soaked trees hanging almost down to the ground. The few cattle who remained grazing looked like sepulchral shadows in the all enveloping gloom. The cars had their fog-lights on, exacerbating the thickness of the mist with their exhausts.

Now, in Worcester Park she would never have let a day like this get her down. If it wasn't a day on which she worked she would ring Pauline or Angela or another mate. Or maybe she'd take the tube up to the West End either alone or with one of the girls. They might have lunch at Selfridges or Dickins and Jones, and trail merrily along Regent Street or Oxford Street, returning replete and happy to get the meal ready in time for family dinner, full of gossip and chat about the day in town.

Helen finished her ironing aware that there loomed a terrible gap in the day. It was still only eleven and the whole day stretched in front of her, the minutes leadenly ticking by.

John had chided her for not taking an interest in the garden. But there was so much to *do*. Muriel said it needed a good turning over, possibly with an excavator, and it did. Anyway now she couldn't possibly do anything before the spring. With occasional night-time frosts the ground was too hard.

68

Oh God the *spring* – at least five months away. They were not even properly into winter.

She took the neat piles of ironing and put them in the airing cupboard. She put away the iron and the ironing board and switched off the TV. She would probably put it on again in a short while but first she would make some coffee and do the housework. It was necessary, vital, to take a grip on herself. Every day she did out one of the rooms and today it was the turn of Meg's bedroom.

She switched on the kettle and the telephone rang. She stood upright as though she'd received a shock, as though it was the very *last* thing she expected to hear. But why on earth, in this modern age, *shouldn't* someone ring her at – she glanced at the clock on the wall – just after eleven in the morning?

Maybe it was John to say he'd changed his mind about the car. Maybe he had a surprise up his sleeve and had even found an old one for her! But nevertheless she went slowly to the phone knowing that on these depressing sorts of days what she dreaded most was the silence.

"Hello?" she said speaking rather loudly into the receiver which she had snatched up.

There was a silence; but it wasn't that hollow silence. Someone was on the end of the line. But she knew that this person, whoever it was, would speak, was collecting his or her thoughts because maybe of the off-putting brusqueness of her tone.

"Hello?" she said again, rather more gently this time.

"Is that er . . ." a very old voice was at the other end of the line, difficult at the moment to tell whether it was a man or a woman. "Is that . . . have you lost a cat?"

"A cat!" Helen gasped, her mind rapidly running back over the last weeks. It seemed now such a long time ago. "Yes of course. We lost a cat . . . a tabby, female, spayed, about three years old."

"Oh!" The voice sounded resigned. "Then I think I

have your cat. I've had her for some weeks. I thought she was a stray. She just wandered into my house and seemed quite content to settle down. Didn't want to leave. I put her out several times but she came back, so I decided to adopt her."

"Oh how *kind*. I'm so sorry. But we love her too." Helen's voice was almost pulsating with joy. "Her name is Skittles."

"Skittles. How quaint. I called her 'puss'. Not very original, I'm afraid." The voice of the very old lady cracked.

"But how did you . . . well how did you find *us*?"

"Someone told me that there was a card in the post office. I never read them I'm afraid. It's been there some time. I think about a month."

"Maybe longer." Helen was trying very hard to remember exactly when it was Skittles had disappeared. Of course for some days they had been unaware that she had gone.

"I think she's been *here* about six weeks; but I have tried to telephone you in the last week or so and I've never been able to get through. There was a funny hollow sound on the line as though someone was there. I reported my phone out of order and now it seems to be all right."

"Oh my goodness!" Helen's hand fluttered to her breast. The relief was almost too much . . . the cat found and the odd behaviour of the telephone explained. This was why she could ring John at work or he could ring her; why she could hear her own mother from Torremolinos and Pauline from Worcester Park; why Muriel could get through from the other side of the road. And she'd thought the place was *haunted*.

Suddenly all her fears and anxieties seemed to dissolve and she could have laughed aloud, only she didn't because the woman on the other end of the phone really *would* have thought she was mad.

"Look, may I come and see if it is Skittles? I don't want

to get too excited. I mean it may not be. She really is my daughter's cat and it would be such a thrill to have her here when she got home."

"Of course," the old lady said rather tremulously and, in halting tones, gave her instructions as to how to reach her cottage.

It was an old, picturesque thatched house past the post office at the far end of the village, quite a walk from the modern estate at the top of the hill. It was the sort of place people who lived in towns dreamed of possessing in the country. In summer it would be covered with clematis and old roses, Compassion or Albertine, and now smoke came out of the chimney and lights gleamed though its old, shiny windows.

As she came up the garden path the front door opened and a very old lady with snow-white hair stood on the doorstep peering out. She wore a cardigan and skirt, round her neck a row of probably very good pearls.

"Have you come a long way?" she said with a smile, stepping back as Helen approached her. "Haven't you a car?"

They shook hands on the doorstep, Helen feeling out of breath and strangely strung up and apprehensive.

"We live at the top of the hill."

"Oh that new estate? I've never been there. They say it is very nice. Very expensive houses."

"This is *much* nicer," Helen said looking around. "It's beautiful."

"I've lived here all my life," the old lady said, leading the way inside. "It was my mother's cottage and she left it to me." She paused, kneading her very thin, arthritic hands one into the other. "I was widowed early in the war. My husband was a lieutenant in the Navy."

"Oh I'm sorry. Did you have children?"

The old lady paused. Then, her voice so faint Helen

71

could scarcely hear it, she said, "We had a son; but he passed away too."

"Oh how *sad*," Helen said feelingly.

"Yes, it was. Very sad. I was all on my own, but my mother was glad to have me. Glad of the company. Now you must come and see . . ." they both stared at each other rather shyly, "see if it is indeed your cat."

Helen walked into the sitting room and knew immediately that it was Skittles curled up with her face in her tail, paws crossed in front of her. There was a log fire in the grate and the room radiated that special sort of warmth and comfort that cottages have, that special sort of air of tranquillity and repose. There were comfy low chairs covered in chintz, and a long sofa that ran almost the length of one of the walls on which there was knitting and some magazines. Helen wished they too could have had a real fire, but there wasn't even a fireplace.

She went over to the chair by the fire and, bending down, lightly touched Skittles, gently stroking her fur towards her tail. Suddenly her eyes filled with tears as the cat looked up, blinked and gently broke into a deeply throttled purr.

"Oh *Skittles*." Helen sat down and scooped the cat up into her lap. "Oh Skittles . . . did we treat you *very* badly?"

"Oh dear," the old lady said watching Helen try so hard to keep back the tears. "I see you're very upset. I'm sure you *didn't* treat her badly—"

"Oh no, no," Helen said hastily, "not physically I assure you. We *adored* her; but we'd recently moved and I don't think she settled."

"Cats hate moving," the old lady agreed. "By the way, my name's Rita Markham."

"And mine's Helen Tempest." Helen smiled self-consciously.

Skittles now tried to wriggle off Helen's lap and Helen thought it was somehow important that the cat should stay; that Skittles should want her and want to come back with her, so she applied some pressure to try and keep her on her lap, all of which was observed by the wily old perspicacious Mrs Markham.

"I should let her go," she said. "Maybe she's had a bit of a shock too. Didn't you try and find her when she disappeared?"

"Of course we did! Only it was some days before we realized she had really disappeared."

Mrs Markham's eyes registered steely disapproval.

"I mean," Helen went on, "we also took some time to settle down. My husband has a new job in Yeovil, an important and demanding one, and the children – we have a boy and a girl – were at a new school. But when we realized that she really had gone of *course* we did everything we could to find her. Looked in the shed," Helen gulped, remembering the shock of that awful day, "all the places where she might have hidden. Then, finally, I put a notice in the post office."

Skittles roamed restlessly around the room as if aware of the importance she had suddenly acquired in the lives of the two people present. Then she paused in front of the sofa where Mrs Markham sat, looked up, flicked her tail and jumped on to the old lady's lap. She turned around a couple of times and then settled down and, head stretched on her paws, appeared to go to sleep. But to Helen it seemed as though the cat surreptitiously was watching *her*.

Mrs Markham gazed at the cat for a moment and then gently began to stroke her. "I shall miss her," she said. "I have come to love her—"

"Maybe we could get another cat?" Helen said impulsively, wondering only later what she would have done if Mrs Markham had agreed.

"Oh *no*," Mrs Markham went with the placid stroking, "she's yours. You said she was your daughter's?" She

73

looked quickly up at Helen, who nodded. "Then your daughter will miss her and you must have her back."

Later that day Helen trudged down the hill again to Mrs Markham's cottage with the cat basket to pick up Skittles, but somehow also with a heavy heart because she knew all too clearly that Skittles, beloved family pet, for some reason preferred where she was and didn't really want to come home. Helen had imagined that the eyes that had observed her so closely were wary and unfriendly.

Finally Skittles was persuaded into the basket while Mrs Markham stood to one side looking nervous and agitated. Skittles didn't settle in her basket but sat staring angrily around, tail waving wildly.

"Well, she's been very happy here." Helen, red-faced, finally closed and secured the door of the basket. "That's obvious. Thank you very much. You must come and see her. I'll get my husband to drive you up." She walked to the door aware of how heavy the cat basket was and what a long way she had to go. She stood on the threshold, looking at the old lady who was trying unsuccessfully to hide her sadness.

"Thank you *so* much."

"Take care." Mrs Markham's kindly face creased with concern. "And take care of the cat."

"Oh I *will*." Helen clutched the basket firmly.

"Don't let her out," Mrs Markham went on, "and if you do, grease her paws. For some reason, I never know why, they say it will always keep a cat straying from its home."

Chapter Five

Pauline Burns was a lively, articulate lady of about the same age as Helen. She had worked for a number of years for the social services as a carer, someone who went into the homes of the elderly or the disabled and helped them to cope with life, made it a little more comfortable and easier for them.

She was a handsome, rather buxom artificial blonde, everybody's idea of a capable, happy-go-lucky person; and yet her own life had not been without its dark side. Her mother had committed suicide and her first child had Downs Syndrome, and died at the age of five of a congenital heart weakness.

Helen had been Pauline's lifeline and she missed her, so much. The chance to take a week off during the school holidays and visit her in Tip Hollow had been seized and acted upon and now she and Sharon sat in the taxi that was taking them the five miles from Yeovil. She had her arm round Sharon and gazed a little uncomprehendingly at the bleak countryside with its seemingly everlasting pall of mist. She didn't know how anyone could live here permanently. Pauline was a town girl if ever there was one, and involuntarily she shivered as the taxi left the main road and began its climb up the hill towards the village.

"Don't know how they can bear it here do you?" she asked brushing back a stray piece of hair from Sharon's brow and looking at her tenderly: her anchor, the one positive thing in her life. "So *far* from anywhere," she murmured, turning again to gaze out of the window at the bleakness of the rural scene. Sharon dolefully followed her mother's gaze. She missed Meg as much as Pauline missed Helen, and had hardly been able to sleep at nights because of the excitement at the thought of seeing her best friend again.

Although a town girl, born and bred, like her mother, she didn't quite share her mother's view of the countryside. Anything to be with Meg once again.

"It's not *bad*," she said pouting. Then, "Maybe they'll come back?"

Her mother looked at her. "*That's* not likely. Mind you, I don't think Helen is all that happy here. In fact I know she's not but, of course, it's John who has the work. It's the *money* that talks, my dear, and the security," and she flung her arm round Sharon again and pressed her closely to her side.

The journey was quite short. Up the hill between the vaulted avenue of trees, on to the village with the stream running along one side, across the bridge and then up the narrow, winding road.

"Know where it is?" the cabbie called over his shoulder.

"No!" Pauline shouted back. "But it's number fourteen."

"Fourteen, right." The driver slowed down and, one by one, they scanned the number plates on the gate posts of the houses set well back from the road. Pauline was impressed.

"Nice," she murmured. "Quite a step up from Worcester Park." Every house was set in its own bit of garden, and in the background were the trees that crested the brow of the hill running down into a pleasant wood alongside it.

"This is it," the driver called, and abruptly put his foot on the brake throwing Pauline and Sharon forward.

Pauline looked up at the house. It was just like the others, though she could tell that each one was a little different from its neighbour. It was built of red brick with a flashy red-tiled roof, a white wooden porch and a brass lamp at either side of the front door. The front garden was not as well tended as the others on the estate. In fact it bore a look of neglect. And, despite the fresh net curtains at the windows, the newish white paint on the woodwork, she thought there was something a little forlorn about the house itself, something impermanent, unwelcoming. Hard to say quite what. Involuntarily she shivered once again.

"This it?" Sharon asked looking up at her mother.

"I think so." Pauline nodded firmly and seized the holdall on the floor in front of her, the carrier bags containing late Christmas presents, Sharon's much loved teddy which she never went anywhere without.

"Looks nice," Sharon said, tumbling out of the taxi in front of her mother. From the side of the house the wind whistled keenly, reminding them it was the depth of winter. Pauline leaned forward to pay the cabbie.

"How much?" she asked and, as she counted out the notes, the door opened and Meg, followed by Helen, rushed out of the house and down the garden path.

The girls flew into each other's arms first; the two women stopped and stared. It seemed so long. Then they too embraced. With a wave the cabbie drove off and Pauline stared after him over the shoulder of her companion, thinking somehow that it was like severing all links with the outside world.

"Well you're *here*." Helen took a step back, looking Pauline up and down. "At last!"

"We made it." Pauline managed a cheery smile. "Lovely house," she said.

"Like it?"

"Much better than number nine."

Nine Lovelace Avenue had been rather cramped, with two decent sized bedrooms and one that was so small it was hardly more than a box room.

"Well," Helen put her head on one side, "it's certainly bigger."

The women linked arms, Helen carrying the holdall, and made their way up the path to the house, the two girls having preceded them.

"I'm so sorry we couldn't meet you. John had to go somewhere – Bristol I think – and couldn't possibly let us have the car."

"That's OK. But you must feel awfully cut off here without one." Pauline paused for a moment, as if revising her first impression, and looked around. "No buses?"

"One a day, but it leaves at nine in the morning."

"How primitive."

"Most people have two cars, of course."

"You'd think with John's salary—"

"Oh you know he's *mean*. Always has been. He thinks it's a needless expense."

Helen closed the door behind them and the house seemed to envelop them. Pauline was aware of an odd sense of oppression. It was quite a large, light, airy house and the open-plan lounge-dining room beckoned. But it was chilly. Of course it was a chilly day.

"Don't you have the heating on?" she asked looking at Helen.

"Oh dear, are you cold?" Helen, concerned, ran to the radiator under the window and put her hand on it. "Piping hot. I insist that in weather like this we have the heating on all day. John . . . well you know him . . ." She gave Pauline a meaningful glance. "I'll make us coffee and you'll warm up in no time. Actually," she studied her watch, "it's time for lunch. Are sandwiches—"

"Sandwiches and coffee would be fine." Pauline gave her a wide grin.

"And a proper meal tonight, of course. John will be back about seven. Jake's away though, on a Scout survival expedition in the Lake District."

Upstairs the two girls babbled away noisily.

"It must *seem* strange here?" Helen watched her friend closely.

"It's a *lovely* house," Pauline responded quickly, "no question. Ever so big." She felt awkward, odd. Of course they hadn't seen each other for nearly six months, though they spoke weekly on the telephone, sometimes more often. "It's just that well," she sank into a chair and lit a cigarette, "I don't know that I'd like to live somewhere so remote. Out of the way." She gestured through the haze towards the window. "I mean do you *know* anybody round here?"

Helen sank on to the chair opposite, clasping her knees. "Not a soul really. They all work. They're also mostly a bit older. The village, of course, is out of the way and the people there are older too. Very few children. People come to retire you know. There's quite a nice woman opposite, but she's not young. I mean she's retired. I wouldn't call her a soul mate."

"It *was* a mistake wasn't it?" Pauline edged closer to the rim of the chair and gazed at her friend.

"*I* think it was a mistake," Helen said, "to come so far out of town, and I think John thinks so too, now, especially now that the winter is here. Five miles isn't far, but without a car it is – especially all those hills."

She got up and went to the kitchen followed by Pauline who looked round appreciatively.

"You've got all the mod cons. Everything you need."

"Exactly." Helen nodded vigorously as if to console herself about something. "More space than at number nine."

"Dishwasher, washing machine, microwave," Pauline intoned, "and I *like* the breakfast bar. I've always wanted one."

"Oh it *couldn't* be better appointed. The people before were," she paused, "well, he was an architect. They did up the place beautifully. Despite that," she gazed around hugging herself, "it's not quite a home, is it? It hasn't a homely *feel*."

"Well *I* didn't want to say anything. And it's far too soon . . ." Pauline stubbed out her cigarette in the sink. "Of course it's a chilly day. One feels it, after the town."

"But it's always like that here." Helen's voice was plaintive. "I can never get the house *warm*."

"Is it damp?" Pauline stared at her.

"Oh no it's not damp. It's just that . . . well . . ." She looked suddenly despairing, lost, and leaned for a second against Pauline.

"You don't like it here, do you, love?" Pauline said thoughtfully stroking her shoulders. "You're not happy? Can't say I blame you really," she said looking round. "It's not the sort of place I'd like to live in myself."

Pauline lay in the dark listening to the sounds from the bedroom next door. Helen and John arguing, trying to keep the noise down but not quite succeeding.

Pauine switched on the bedside light and looked at the clock. Nearly one. The time seemed to drag. It had all day. Gone so slowly, perhaps, because there was nothing to do. In the afternoon it had settled into a steady downpour and they were cooped up inside, unable to get out and look round the place which Pauline would have liked, just to get *away* from the somehow claustrophobic atmosphere of the house. Yet outdoors hadn't really seemed any more appealing. She'd spent a lot of time looking out on to the desolate scene, smoking cigarettes, while Helen poured out her heart about her frustration, her sense of emptiness, her fear.

Pauline lit a cigarette as the buzz of voices next door continued and propped herself up against the pillows. It was a bright, recently decorated room with chintzy curtains and whitewood furniture, none of it very expensive, but nor was it particularly cheap. Helen had replaced some of the furniture she'd had in Worcester Park and there was a new neutral carpet on the floor. There were two single beds in the spare room and a bedside table with lamps in between. Quite nice. Like a hotel really. Not cosy, but then Helen had never been a particularly cosy sort of person. The house in Worcester Park hadn't been cosy either.

But it certainly never had this chill. Maybe it was the country. Pauline turned to the bedside table and flicked her ash into the empty matchbox she was using as an ashtray.

John hadn't seemed terribly pleased to see her; but then he was never a man to show much emotion. Not universally popular in Worcester Park, not very much liked, but then not particularly well *known*. Not a mixer; the sort of man who kept himself to himself; canny, silent, rather remote. A cold fish, John. And very odd those war games he played; childish.

In front of her on the wall was a large map of the Battle of Naseby in 1645 which, according to the short legend at its base, had effectively sealed the fate of poor King Charles I. There was an engraving showing the disposition of the forces of the King and those of Cromwell who put the monarchists to flight leaving, it was said, a trail of bodies all the way to Leicester.

Pauline shuddered and pulled the duvet closer round her. It was, indeed, bloody cold now and she thanked heaven for the electric overblanket. The heating went off sharp at ten p.m. Trust John to insist on that. Went on at seven a.m., off at ten p.m., and was carefully graded during the winter months.

Pauline lit a fresh cigarette from the stub of the old, and blew smoke into the air. This obsession with battles in one seemingly so mild and, well, dull, was one of the curious contradictions about him. Helen had firmly restricted the number of maps he was allowed to put up in the new house; but there were two in the hall, two on the landing and one here in the spare room. Beautifully framed, but what a hobby, *and* the bookcase full of books on military history as well as the paperback romances which were Helen's staple fare.

Well, she tried to cheer herself up, it *was* only the first day. She didn't go away much, and maybe she felt strange. Sharon had settled in all right and was sleeping in the bottom bunk in Meg's room. Occasionally from there came the sound of stifled giggles. Maybe they were listening to the row between the two adults in the room in between.

There was one thing that was for sure. She wasn't going to stay here a week. Already an afternoon and an evening seemed too long. It was one of those places you felt you wanted to get away from, almost straight away.

She inhaled and blew another cloud of thick smoke, hastily dispersing it with her hand, as though someone were watching her.

And someone was . . . his face clearly etched in the smoke: a sad, rather careworn face, impossible to say how old. It stared down at her so clearly that she sat bolt upright in bed, her heart pounding. Then she lay back and closed her eyes and, of course, when she opened them again there was nothing there. There were not even any lingering traces of the smoke that had undoubtedly formed the apparition, or what she thought was an apparition. Trick of the eye.

The room was colder still. Even the bed was cold.

She knew now that her nerves, always a strong point, needed in her job, were getting the better of her; but already she dreaded tomorrow.

Pauline awoke in the morning and listened to the silence. It was light outside so it must have been after eight. She looked at her watch. It was. From the glow round the window it looked as though it was a sunny day.

She lay for a moment reorientating herself, trying to

recall the fears and anxieties of the night before. Now a good sleep, the possibility of sun and a new day, seemed to banish the gloom of the night before and her habitual optimism returned.

She got up, drew aside the curtains and welcomed the bright sunshine flooding into the room. It was a cold, crisp day and a frost still lingered on the fields beyond the house.

Pauline now saw the countryside with a very different eye from the day before. The journey, the anxiety of packing up and getting away, had tired her. In fact she very rarely got away, tied down to her job by financial necessity and also concern for those in her care, who seldom if ever took holidays.

But she had slept well and if she had dreams she didn't remember them. She looked forward to the day, the holiday, making the best of what really, now that she saw it in the sunshine, was glorious countryside, and in the company of one of her oldest and best friends.

She opened the bedroom door and listened. All was silent. John, of course, would have gone to work and, creeping along the corridor and turning the handle of the girls' room, she found it in darkness. They were still fast asleep. Doubtless after giggling most of the night and exchanging stories they would sleep until mid-morning, if not noon. She closed the door as quietly as she had opened it and went along to the bathroom where she brushed her teeth. Then tugging her streaked blonde hair into its habitual ponytail she descended the staircase to the hall.

"Anyone there?" she called opening the kitchen door.

Helen, her gown wrapped tightly around her, was sitting at the table, a mug of tea in front of her, turning over the pages of the *Daily Mail*. She looked up with a startled expression as the door opened and then her features relaxed when she saw who it was.

"Oh it's you," she said with a smile brushing back her dark curls.

"Who did you think it was?" Pauline came into the kitchen groping in her pocket for her cigarettes.

"Oh you know." As Helen leaned back in the chair Pauline saw how tired she looked, her eyes puffy with dark lines under the bags.

Puzzled, the feeling of wellbeing slowly evaporating, Pauline went over to the kettle, filled it and turned it on, put a teabag in a mug.

"Mind if I make tea?" she asked as the kettle began to boil.

"Oh of course not." Helen jumped up guiltily. "I'm a lousy hostess. I was going to make you a cup and bring it up to you in bed." She glanced at the clock on the kitchen wall. "I didn't realize how late it was."

"Didn't sleep well?" Pauline grimaced sympathetically and, adding milk to her tea, brought it over to the table and sat opposite her friend, producing a cigarette from the pack.

"Do you mind me smoking so early in the day?"

"Of course not."

"John gone?" Pauline lit her cigarette, took a large welcome gulp of smoke and exhaled.

"Long ago. He always leaves early. Likes to be first at the office."

"I couldn't help, well, hearing the pair of you quarrelling last night." Pauline stuffed her cigarettes back in her pocket. "I hope John isn't put out having me here."

"Oh that wasn't about *you*. I think he's quite glad you're here. It's just, well, we're like that every night. We both seem to nurse all the resentments of the day and they come pouring out when we're in bed."

"Bad as that?"

"Bad!" Helen nodded and, with a swift movement of her hand across her face, seemed to wipe away a tear.

"But it wasn't like that before?" Pauline looked puzzled.

"It wasn't as *bad* as that before," Helen corrected

her. "It hasn't been good for some time. We've been slowly drifting apart. No doubt about that. I think John imagined a change would do us good but to come here . . . to this," she paused and looked helplessly around her, "to this isolated, desolate place was the worst thing we could have done. It made the situation between us far worse. To buy a repossessed house, where people were *unhappy*, was asking for trouble. Well, wasn't it?"

Pauline smoked silently for a moment, not quite knowing how to reply. She was used to confidences, to unhappy, often lonely people, unburdening themselves on her. But they were usually older than Helen. Much older. They were usually elderly people whose families neglected them, who had few friends and not enough to occupy themselves. Helen, on the other hand, was a woman of her age, an attractive, vibrant woman. She had never seen her in this sort of mood ever before and it shocked her.

"I thought you got on well. Not like Jim and me."

"I suppose it was *because* I was so concerned about you and Jim that I didn't talk much about us. Anyway," Helen took a sip of tea, "I never thought about it all that much. I had a lot to do. I thought we went the way most couples go. You drift apart after a time. It's nature isn't it? Inevitable. Oh there was nothing seriously wrong—"

"But there is now?"

"Seriously?" Helen swept aside her hair again. "I don't know. I think it's a difficult time. A bad phase. Moving in the winter was stupid, to a remote place where there is hardly any transport, to a spot like this, isolated on a hill. Most of the neighbours are out at work all day. Maybe that's why I think there's something wrong with the house. I am sure a psychiatrist would be able to explain it all." Helen gave a wan smile and gulped down her tea.

Pauline stared around her. She wasn't so sure. The sun had gone in, and all at once the landscape looked grey and desolate, the ghostly outlines of the trees vaguely discernible through the mist. It was quite a rapid change of climate from a few moments before and she went to the kitchen window and stood there, peering out.

"Does the weather change so quickly here? It was bright sunshine a few moments ago." She looked over her shoulder at Helen, who was making more tea.

"We're on a hill. Yes, it does seem to change quickly. Sunshine one moment, rain or mist the next. I never notice it really."

"But don't you think it's important?" Pauline turned round. "You know if it's sunny all the time one feels quite happy. When it rains—"

"Yes, but it never *is* sunny all the time is it? I mean not in this country."

"There's a disorder called SAD . . . people affected by the weather. Something syndrome. I forget quite what the name of it is now."

"I'm not affected by the weather." Helen slapped the table firmly with her hand. "I'm affected by *this* place. *This* house. That's what gets me down."

Pauline sat down again still gazing around her.

"There is actually nothing *wrong* with the house, Helen," she said in her best 'carer' manner. "It's a very nice house. I wouldn't mind a house like it. You have plenty of room which you never had before. You've got a 'thing' about it. It's completely illogical. You must realize that."

"People were unhappy here . . . Imagine having your home taken away."

"So?" Pauline looked at her and lit another cigarette. "People are unhappy in loads of places. You should meet some of the people I look after. People *die* in houses. That doesn't mean they hang around to haunt those who come after them. For all I know the previous occupants of my house were unhappy. Or yours at number nine. If you and John weren't getting on so well

86

lately do you think that is affecting the people who live there now?"

"I don't know." Helen's features softened. "You're right. It *does* all seem a bit silly. Care for some toast?" she said getting up.

Suddenly she seemed to have perked up, as if having her friend to confide in, to share her troubles with, made her feel better. Much better.

But Pauline, for some obscure reason, felt glum again. She wondered if she could really stay out the week, or if she'd have to find some excuse to go home. Whatever she said to Helen, the place definitely oppressed her.

Helen finished making toast, produced pots of jam and marmalade, and the women were tucking into their breakfast and more tea when the front door bell chimed. Helen started, the stricken expression returning to her face again.

"Who could that be?" she said.

"Search me! Maybe the milkman? The post?"

"People so seldom call here."

"Cooeee," a voice cried and as the kitchen door opened Muriel popped her head round. "Oh, so sorry Helen, I didn't know you had a visitor. The door was open and I—"

"Come in, come in," Helen called, jumping up. "This is my friend Pauline from London. Pauline this is Muriel who lives opposite."

"How do you do?" Pauline extended a hand.

"Nice to meet you," Muriel said, looking apologetic.

"It's an awful time to pop in, Helen." She pointed towards the table. "I see you haven't yet had your breakfast. If I'd known you had a friend—"

"Oh sit down and have a cup of tea. Or would you prefer coffee?"

Muriel glanced at the clock on the wall. "I won't have anything, thanks. I must be off. But I wondered if you . . . and your friend," she glanced across at Pauline, "would like to come to Bournemouth for the day tomorrow? I mean, if you don't—"

"But we'd *love* to," both women chorused together.

"I've never been to Bournemouth," Pauline said excitedly. "That *would* be lovely." Then she put a hand to her mouth, guiltily looking at Helen. "What about the girls?"

"Girls?" Muriel looked blank.

"I've a daughter too. Same age as Meg."

"They're very welcome." Momentarily Muriel looked nonplussed. "But it will be a bit of a squeeze."

"Oh! I'll sit in the back with the girls," Pauline said cheerfully. "They're both slim."

"Oh! That *is* something to look forward to." Helen appeared quite animated. "Thanks *ever* so much. The January sales will be on."

"Exactly . . . anyway I must trot off to Salisbury now. I've got business there."

"Business?" Pauline looked at her. "Are you in business?"

"No I'm a retired schoolteacher, but I like looking up old records."

"What sort of old records?"

"Places. Salisbury is very old. You must have heard of Sarum?"

"You might try looking up 'Hollow'." Helen gave a sarcastic laugh.

Muriel, also with a laugh, got up. "Oh I know all about Tip Hollow. It was the first thing I did when I moved here. It is in fact a very ancient settlement, probably Bronze Age. This hill where we are now was almost certainly an ancient burial ground. It was once Barrow Hill, and a barrow is a place where people were buried long long ago. Now I mustn't chatter. I'll look forward to seeing you tomorrow. Is about ten OK?"

"Ten is fine," Helen said. "We'll make sure the girls are up by that time. I'll come and see you out—"

"Oh don't *bother*." Muriel looked at Pauline who smiled at her politely.

"See you tomorrow Pauline."

"That *will* be lovely."

When the two women had disappeared through the door Pauline took the mugs over to the sink. Then she turned on the tap and, once again, stood staring out at the landscape. The mist had cleared and it looked as though the sun was struggling to get out again. She began to wash the cups and plates when she heard footsteps behind her and turned to see that Helen had returned and was putting away the jars in the cupboard.

"Seems a nice woman," Pauline said.

"Very nice. Of course she's not our generation but she's very nice. A kind person."

Pauline took up a towel and began wiping the dishes. "Does she know how you feel about the house?"

"Yes, though we haven't mentioned it for ages. She thinks it's silly. Doesn't believe that houses have feelings. Well it *is* silly isn't it? Really?" Helen had a wistful look as though she was dying to be reassured.

"Nevertheless I thought it very tactless to say that this was once a burial ground."

"Oh?" Helen looked surprised. "Why?"

"Well it's a bit sinister isn't it? I mean when you come to think." Pauline put the cups on a shelf above the sink to drain. "If you're already nervous about the place . . ."

"But you see *she* doesn't think like that. She's far too sensible and I," Helen sat down heavily planting her feet in front of her and studied them, "I must be sensible too. Houses *can't* have feelings can they?"

"They can have atmosphere." Pauline also sat down. "A house can have a 'friendly' feel . . . but it can't 'feel' itself, can it?" She scratched her head. She was about to go on when a sudden noise seemed to erupt from overhead. "My God what on *earth* is that?"

89

From upstairs came the sound of angry shouts, the words difficult to make out.

"I *believe* the girls are actually quarrelling." Pauline looked at Helen in amazement. "I never knew them do that did you?"

Helen shook her head.

Together they dived for the door, ran along the hall where they paused standing at the bottom of the stairs.

"I said it's *my* turn," came Meg's voice raised in anger.

"Mine!" from Sharon.

"Mine!"

"Mine!"

All with mounting anger and hostility. The two mothers went quietly up the stairs until they reached the landing where they could see the two girls confronting each other outside the bathroom, as each appeared to be trying to get in before the other.

"Girls, girls!" Helen called. "What on earth are you up to?"

"It's *my* turn for the bathroom," screamed Meg.

"It's *mine*," shouted Sharon. "*She* went first last night."

"But what a silly, trivial thing to quarrel about," Helen said angrily trying to separate them. "I never *heard* such a silly thing in my *life*." She took Meg by the arm and angrily pulled her back, opening the bathroom door and indicating to Sharon that she should go through. "Of course, as your guest, Sharon goes first."

"And what a silly thing to make a fuss about." Pauline also looked amazed. "You, who have always been such good friends. I'm ashamed of you both."

Meg looked rebelliously at Sharon who strode into the bathroom and, pausing by the door, made a face at her before quickly shutting the door behind her. Meg wrenched herself from her mother's grasp and, rushing towards it, kicked the door hard with her slippered foot.

"*Meg!*" Helen reached out to smack her, but Pauline restrained her.

"Don't. They were up all night talking. They're tired out." She called through the door, "Sharon don't be long."

"I'll be as long as I like," Sharon shouted back. "All day if I want."

"No you don't, because *we* want to get in too," Pauline said angrily.

"You can use the bathroom next to our bedroom." Helen wearily passed her hand across her forehead. "Really I think I'm beginning to get one of my heads, and the day has scarcely begun."

Chapter Six

Pauline sat at the kitchen table, head bent over the *Daily Mail* which Helen had been leafing through in the morning. It was after lunch and, for once, a sense of calm pervaded the house. The children had settled and were now watching television in Meg's bedroom. Helen had decided, after all, not to have a headache and was tidying herself in the bedroom, preparing for a walk.

Yet Pauline felt unsettled, and trying to induce a sense of calm seemed difficult and, for her, untypical. She was a calm, controlled person which was why she was so good at her job; a person used to coping in difficult situations, restoring order, taking charge.

Her mind was not on the paper, not that there was much to report in the news anyway. She tossed it to one side and, chin balanced on her hand, stared in front of her in the direction of the window, seeing and not seeing.

Suddenly there was a fuzzy, wavy shape in front of her and her eyes quickly refocused. Skittles sat on the outside of the kitchen windowsill peering in, a paw lifted to scratch the surface of the glass.

As Pauline's face broke into a relieved smile Skittles gave a mighty yawn and scratched the window again. Pauline jumped up from the table and went over to open the window for her.

"Hello Skittles," she said drawing her in. "And where have *you* been?"

Skittles gave her the disdainful look of a cat whose mind is on something else. She paused on the edge of the stainless steel sink, looking downwards and then, with feline grace, leapt to the floor and began eagerly to explore the contents of the food bowl. She looked rather dishevelled as though she'd had a night out, a dispute, perhaps many, with another cat. She wound her tail round her body and sank her teeth into the food in the bowl.

Pauline, aware of how cold it was outside and wondering if a walk was a good idea, thankfully shut the window and returned to her chair where she sat watching the cat.

Skittles finished all the food, except for a bit, and then applied herself to the milk in the bowl beside her. She lapped quietly and contentedly for a while. Then she stretched, gazed at Pauline and jumped on to the kitchen table where she started to groom herself, first by the side of her tail, then her backside as far as she could reach, her chest and, finally, licking her paw she rhythmically applied it to her face and behind her ears.

Cats were quite fascinating, Pauline thought; restful, disdainful, mysterious creatures. She wished she had one, but she didn't think it was fair when you were out all day and lived near a busy street.

She sat back in the chair, arms folded, marvelling at the number of times Skittles licked her paw, applying it to the side of her face and up over her ear, the same action repeated over and over, perhaps a hundred times. Was it a futile operation? Did the face really get a wash? Anyway it had a mesmeric effect on the observer. One went into a trance-like state from which it became difficult to rouse oneself.

Suddenly, to her surprise, Skittles, finishing her careful toilet, strolled over to the side of the table and stared amiably at Pauline. Then with a delicate inclination of her head, as if asking permission, she jumped on to Pauline's lap, made several turns and then settled down, with a deep-throated, contented purr.

Pauline felt enormously flattered at this honour and, raising her hand, gently began to stroke her, her long fingers lingering on the beautiful grey markings of a creature whose origins lay deep in antiquity. Skittles responded by stretching, the purr deepening, eyes languorous, her paws kneading Pauline's knee.

Suddenly Skittles raised her head, nostrils quivering. A singularly unpleasant smell pervaded the air. It smelt like sewage, compost, which seemed to increase in intensity.

Skittles' purring ceased abruptly as she jumped on to the floor and began pacing backwards and forwards, her delicate nostrils sniffing the air as if in search of the malodorous substance.

Pauline slowly stood up and followed the movements of the cat. The pungency of the smell almost made her choke and her first instinct was that it came from the drains. She went to the sink and put her nose to the plughole, but it was quite fresh. Skittles seemed to think that the smell came from somewhere in the centre of the room, which Pauline tended to agree with, only it seemed impossible. Feeling increasingly foolish she got on to her knees and sniffed the vinyl covering of the floor, whereupon the smell abruptly seemed to evaporate.

She went to the kitchen door, tested the air. There was the faintest whiff of silage. She was joined by Skittles, who too had decided to step outside and was fastidiously inspecting the drain. No smell there.

Ushering the cat through, Pauline returned to the kitchen, closed the door and the smell seemed more powerful than ever. Skittles, however, appeared to have lost interest, went over to the near-empty bowl, sniffed it, finished the morsel of food she had left in it and then, striding back to the chair Pauline had vacated, jumped on it and curled up to go to sleep.

There was the sound of footsteps running down the stairs and in a moment the door opened and Helen came in dressed in a track suit and trainers. She looked less strained than she had in the morning, but when she saw the expression on Pauline's face she asked "Anything wrong?"

"Awful smell." Pauline raised her nose in the air. "Can't you smell it?"

Helen also dutifully sniffed the air and shook her head. "What kind of smell?"

"Ghastly. Like drains." Pauline sniffed again.

"There *is* a smell," Helen said carefully, "but I think it's from outside." Then seeing the supine figure curled up on the chair she scooped Skittles into her arms.

"*There* you are, you naughty girl. You're always giving me a fright." Skittles, clearly displeased at being disturbed from her slumbers, tried to wriggle out. Finally successful, she regained her place on the chair and Helen tried to sweep the cat hairs off her track suit.

"Out all night?" Pauline smiled.

"She keeps going off. She was once lost for nearly six weeks."

"I remember you saying. Thought you'd lost her." Pauline glanced at herself in the kitchen mirror. "Do I look OK?"

"You look fine. I thought we'd just have a walk in the village and see the old girl who rescued Skittles. I suspect she goes back there from time to time and I'm going to ask her, very politely, *not* to feed the cat."

"That'd be nice." Pauline was puzzled about the rapidly evaporating smell and prowled around as if still seeking the source.

"I tell you it's from outside."

"I thought it was here."

"You're imagining it."

"*And* the cat noticed it." Pauline pointed at Skittles. "She smelt it first and jumped off my knee. Walked around and around with me."

Helen opened the door of the fridge and leaned inside.

95

"All fine here." She sniffed again and shook her head. "It was silage from outside. I hope you're not suggesting bad drains, or that the food is off."

"Oh *Helen*!" Pauline looked flustered. "Forget it." She looked at the clock on the wall, then outside. "Now what about that walk? It will soon be dark. Are you calling the girls?"

"They don't want to come anyway, and there's a film on TV. I think they'll be OK for an hour don't you?"

"I'd think so." Pauline stopped to stroke the cat who, however, ignored her.

Outside it was very cold. A frost that had settled over the ground during the night had not melted. Pauline had on jeans, a thick sweater, boots and a scarf wound round her head. Helen had on a bright cherry-coloured woolly hat which looked nice over her dark hair, and went well with her shining cheeks. They began to walk briskly down the hill towards the village seeming, for once, to have little to say until they reached the bridge and, leaning over the parapet, gazed into the swift flowing waters of the stream.

"Do you think you'll stay here?" Pauline looked sideways at Helen.

"Well not for *ever*. I mean I hope we could move quite soon, but it doesn't look as though there's much of a chance. Why, don't you like it?"

"Frankly I couldn't stand living here, but then I'm not a country woman. I mean I *love* it for a few days." She mimed enthusiastically, gesturing around. "The countryside is beautiful, really lovely. But I'd hate to be," she paused, "so cut off. No car."

"Yes that *is* awful, but I'm working on John. I'll make it so bad for him that in the end he'll have to give in. I'm sure he has the money. He just doesn't want to part with it. I mean I only want a second-hand car after all –

a battered old Mini, something like that. But John says it's a waste of money."

"Well, you want something that won't keep breaking down. I mean I can see John's point about having a fairly decent car."

Helen looked at her.

"I suppose you can hear everything. The walls are so thin."

Pauline felt herself blushing. "I mean, I don't listen deliberately—"

"It's the only time we have to talk about anything in bed at night," Helen sighed, "and then it usually ends in a row. I'm sorry. You must think we're very unhappy."

"I—"

Helen held up a hand. "Let me finish. We're going through a bad phase. I'll admit that."

"But it's lasting a rather *long* time isn't it? I mean you've been here six months."

"Sure. It is rather long. You know what they say – divorce, moving, bereavement; they all rate about the same on the trauma scale. Then I had the stupid hang-up about the house. I'm trying to overcome it, really I am. But then you go on about smells—"

"But a smell has nothing to do with the *house*."

"You made it sound as though it had. A musty smell, like death, decay. I have smelt it, actually, but I think it came from outside. I *wanted* it to come from outside."

"It's nothing to do with the house." Pauline was positive.

"I don't *like* the house. I never did."

"Then it was really stupid to agree to move here."

"I had no option. Frankly I don't think I'd have liked anywhere. I didn't want to leave Worcester Park. Maybe I used the excuse about people being unhappy in the house, though I did care that it had been repossessed. I know *nothing* about the Beckets except that Muriel says they were always having rows . . ." She smiled

97

ruefully as she saw the expression on Pauline's face. "OK really *bad* rows, not like ours which are really little tiffs. The Beckets' rows raised the roof. Maybe the Beckets were just never happy people, whereas we . . ." Helen appeared to consider the matter for a moment or two, "well I think we were a pretty ordinary family. Usual ups and downs."

"At least you and John stayed together," Pauline said encouragingly.

"Exactly and I think we will. We've been married nearly fifteen years. I see no reason to change and I know he doesn't, despite the bickering. He told me last night that he intends to try to move within a year. He's going to put it to his boss who is due to visit in the summer, by which time he will have been here nearly a year."

They threw some pebbles into the water, crossed to the other side of the bridge and walked slowly along the main street. It was really a very pretty village, the sort one saw and admired on innumerable picture postcards. There was a row of thatched cottages with overhanging eaves and neat grass verges, a pub, the Cross and Keys, which was half timbered, and then the post office which had a double-fronted window and also served as the village shop. Outside were boxes of fruit and vegetables, a few rather bedraggled plants which were being sold off.

Helen stopped to cross the road by the post office and Pauline, catching up with her after lingering to look at the wares on offer in the shop window, appeared surprised.

"Skittles comes this far?"

"Yes. I think the old lady encouraged her to stay. Maybe still does. I'm definitely going to tell her to stop."

On the other side of the road, tall banks of fir trees rose steeply up the hill so that the house outside which Helen stopped, seemed half protected by them.

Pauline stood beside her.

"This it?"

Helen nodded, looking puzzled.

"It looks empty, doesn't it?"

"Yes it does." There was no smoke from the chimney and the windows looked as though it was a long time since they'd been cleaned. The tiny leaded panes winked opaquely in the late afternoon sun which prepared to disappear across the valley.

As Helen gazed at the house she felt the house was gazing back at her, that the windows were sightless eyes and the whitewashed exterior the face of a corpse. She opened the garden gate and went up the path, aware of a sense of foreboding, a deep apprehension and fear of the unknown.

The door knocker was festooned with cobwebs and Helen suddenly visualized the latch on the shed the day she'd found the dead cat. Instead of taking the knocker in her hand she stepped to one side and, rubbing the window pane, peered inside.

It was empty, deserted, and looked as though it had been for a very long time.

She knew she must take a grip on herself, not lose control; but she realized that the prickly fear which seemed to freeze her blood was always there, just beneath the surface, needing something like this, like the cat, to rekindle it. She was aware of Pauline standing next to her, and she too leaned forward and rubbed the window pane.

"It looks as though it was been empty for ages." She stepped back and gazed at Helen. "Are you sure this is the place?"

"Pretty sure." Helen tried to keep her voice matter-of-fact. "Of course it *was* some time ago."

"But not *that* long." Pauline peered inside again. "It's festooned with cobwebs."

"Well . . ." Helen pulled her woolly hat well down on her head, as though for warmth, and began to beat her arms with her hands to get the blood running through her veins again.

"Let's ask at the post office," Pauline suggested. "I mean you may be mistaken."

Helen knew she wasn't mistaken, but obediently she walked back down the path in the wake of Pauline, who seemed to have assumed the lead. Pauline held the garden gate open for her and she trotted through and stood in the road, not wanting to look back at the house.

They walked in silence together to the post office and even then Helen loitered outside inspecting the fruit and veg, not wanting to go in. Pauline gave her a friendly shove.

"Go on," she said. "Ask."

The postmistress greeted Helen with her customary smile. It was obvious that although she didn't remember her name she knew who she was.

"Hello," she said. "Did you get your cat back?"

"Oh yes," Helen said nonchalantly. "Ages ago." Then, seeing the look the postmistress gave her, "Sorry I should have told you."

"Oh that's quite all right. When you didn't renew the card I took it out of the window."

Helen looked around as if she were contemplating some purchase. Then she said casually, "I just wondered . . ." she jerked her head in the direction of the old house, "did Mrs Markham move?"

"Mrs Markham?" The postmistress looked puzzled.

"The elderly lady who lived in the cottage."

"Oh Mrs Markham. My goodness I've almost forgotten her. Move, did you say?" She leaned forward and smiled. "She's been dead for years my dear." She put a finger to her mouth as if in deep thought. "Must be at least five years." She called to the back of the shop to some unseen person or persons, "Len, how long since Mrs Markham died?"

Something inaudible came from the back, which the postmistress obligingly interpreted.

"My husband thinks about five years. Her relatives

are still squabbling over the estate so the house remains unsold. Pity really, as it's going to ruin—"

"And no one has lived there since?" Pauline, perceiving that Helen seemed incapable of speech, moved supportively to her friend's side.

"Oh no, dear. It's damp, they say the floorboards are rotting. Now is there anything I can get you?"

"A pound of carrots please," Helen said, putting her hand in her pocket and mechanically producing her purse. "Oh and a pound of sugar."

The postmistress bustled about while Helen remained staring in front of her. Pauline – calm, practical Pauline, followed the postmistress to the back of the shop.

"Is there another cottage like it?"

"Well there's one up the road." The woman looked puzzled. "There are two or three actually; the row of thatched cottages you must have passed a few yards back."

"But they're not exactly *like* it are they? Like Mrs Markham's?"

"Not really, but they're the only other thatched cottages in the village."

The woman returned to the counter, weighed the carrots and put them on the bench in front of her.

"And sugar?" She looked at Helen.

"Yes please."

"There's no other cottage that stands on its own *anywhere*?" Pauline pursued, in an effort to try to unravel the mystery.

"No, not that I know. Perhaps another village." With a trace of impatience she put the sugar and carrots in a large brown paper bag and rang up the items on the till.

"That will be £1.73 please. The carrots weighed a little bit over the pound. Is that all right?"

"That's fine thank you." Helen carefully took the purchases and tucked them under her arm.

101

"So glad you found the pussy," the postmistress called after her. "You see you take care of her now."

Outside in the street Pauline caught up with Helen, who seemed to be walking in a daze. Pauline tucked her arm through that of her friend.

"It couldn't have been the cottage," Pauline said, squeezing her arm.

"It was. I know it was."

"But it's so bizarre!"

"And the name of the woman?" Helen stopped and looked at her. "I'd hardly make it up would I?"

"There must be *some* explanation." Pauline glanced back along the darkening street and saw that the cottage was now shrouded in a fine mist.

"This woman phoned me and said she had a cat. Someone had *told* her there was a postcard in the post office. All that was real. Not dreamed up. I went to pick Skittles up. I went twice because I returned to get the cat basket. I went *back* to the cottage which was prettily furnished with a fire in the grate and a dear old lady . . . *and* the cat."

"Such things don't happen." Pauline tenderly placed an arm around Helen's shoulders.

"Such things *do* happen, are happening," Helen said in a quiet voice. Then she gazed up at the puzzled face of the woman beside her. "Unless I'm mad. Do you think I'm mad?"

"Of course I don't," Pauline said, hugging her. "I never knew anyone less mad. I don't know how or why, but I think you made a mistake . . . got the wrong place. You've had a stressful time—"

"That's the same as saying you don't believe me."

"I do. I do believe you . . ." and Pauline paused not knowing what, in all honesty, she could say.

John said moodily, "She never used to have these headaches."

102

Helen was lying down and they were sitting at the kitchen table having a snack supper: poached eggs on toast. John had had a couple of stiff whiskies beforehand and Pauline a large sherry. Pauline felt that her holiday, to which she had so looked forward, was going badly wrong and she almost longed to get back to the normality of Worcester Park again. Hard to believe she'd only been here two days. It seemed like a week; no, longer, a month.

"I never remember her having headaches," Pauline acknowledged. "Has she had many?"

"Only since we've been here."

"She's not happy, is she?"

"No." John shook his head. "I think it's just a matter of time, settling down."

"She's absolutely nothing to *do*, John."

"She's plenty to do." John gestured round. "This place really could do with decorating from top to bottom. Other people do it. Why can't Helen turn her hand to something useful? Then there's the garden . . . she didn't touch that. I really don't know what she *does* with the time."

"She'd like a proper job, and I don't just mean housework or gardening. Helen was never that sort of person – DIY I mean, was she?"

"Well she could learn. She could try."

"But why *should* she?"

"Because we haven't any money, that's why," John said angrily, getting up and starting to pace the kitchen. "Moving is a very expensive business, children are expensive. I've never made a lot of money, and because of the family I haven't been able to save, not much anyway – a bit put by, but nothing that would enable me to splash out on moving within a year, or a car or whatever else it is she wants. We have to be very careful. In these hard times one never knows how long one can hang on to a job."

Pauline gazed at him thoughtfully. She had never

before witnessed an outburst of emotion from John, hardly thought he was capable of it. He always seemed a reasonable, even-tempered, extremely dull man. She'd never known what Helen saw in him. At least her ex-husband had a bit of go, even if it did lead him into the wrong direction. He had some sparkle, some fire in his belly.

John Tempest was one of those people it was very easy to forget, hard to recall in retrospect even what they looked like. He was of moderate height, moderate build with nondescript features and mouse-coloured hair going thin on top. He wore glasses which he had a habit of perpetually pushing up his thin nose as if they were too large or too heavy for him. His only hobby or extravagance that anyone knew of was a passion for historical battles, particularly the Civil War in England, and when he lived in Worcester Park he liked to play war games with a few like-minded cronies.

Pauline supposed that John too had to give up a lot of things to come here, live in Dorset and work just over the border in Somerset. Yet he was clearly ambitious because he'd wanted to be a manager. But he was neither happy nor content; neither of them were.

Jake she hadn't seen, obviously because he was away. Meg seemed OK except for these outbursts of temper, which Pauline again couldn't remember before, and which were clearly unsettling her own not too even-tempered daughter Sharon.

Truth to tell she would like to have gone back tomorrow, but how could you suddenly . . . besides how *now* could she desert her great friend who was clearly suffering from some kind of delusion? Maybe on the brink of a nervous breakdown? That was the only thing that Pauline could put this extraordinary happening about the Markham cottage down to.

"Has Helen seen a doctor about her headaches?" she asked, and John paused in his pacing.

"Why should she?"

"Well if she has frequent headaches and she didn't before, it seems logical," Pauline replied tartly.

"Oh I think she's putting it on."

"John!" Pauline got up and pushed her chair angrily to one side. "I *know* Helen and I don't think she *is* putting it on. I think she is sick, and maybe getting sicker. You've been here six months and you say she has frequent headaches which she hadn't had before. Yet you don't seem to *care*. Have you ever considered the possibility she might be seriously ill?"

"Oh don't be silly." But she seemed to have cast doubts in John's unimaginative mind. "Do you really think so?"

"I think she should just be checked out. That's all."

"I'll tell her to see a doctor then," John said grumpily and, looking at his watch, added, "nearly time for the nine o'clock news."

That night Pauline lay awake for a long time acutely aware of the silence all round her. She almost wished for the bickering from the bedroom next door, the giggles from the one beyond.

She lay for a long time with the light out, conscious of an unease, an apprehension that was totally unfamiliar to her, to a woman of her temperament and disposition, without which she would never have held down her sometimes stressful job.

She didn't even dare to put the light on and have a cigarette, in case that strange outline of a human form should once more reappear out of the wreaths of smoke and look sadly down at her.

"I'm terribly sorry," Pauline said, "but Helen's not well."

"Oh dear!" Muriel stood back from the front door and beckoned her visitor in. "Do come in, away from the cold. I'm very sorry to hear that." She led the way into a pleasant sitting room whose windows faced the garden, the front looking on to the Tempests'. "Does that mean the Bournemouth visit is off?"

"I'm afraid so." Pauline looked crestfallen. "I was so looking forward to it, so was she."

"Well couldn't you—"

"Oh I couldn't," Pauline firmly shook her head. "Oh no, it wouldn't be right to leave Helen alone. I'd be too worried." She paused and lowered her voice as if a third party could somehow be listening. "I don't think she's at all well."

Muriel pointed to a chair and, as Pauline sat down, she perched on the arm of the one opposite, her kindly face creased with concern.

"What's the problem?"

"I'm very worried about my friend. I've never seen her like this in all the time I've known her. I think she's having some sort of nervous breakdown." Pauline stared solemnly at the woman in front of her.

"Oh my goodness!" Muriel clasped the pearls over her sensible jumper. "But she always seems well; very bright and friendly when I talk to her. I'm sorry to say it isn't as often as I would like. I'm always so busy. In fact I feel guilty that I don't see enough of her, which was why I suggested the trip today. It must be awful not having a car."

"It is." Pauline nodded vigorously. "She feels terribly isolated. Of course she didn't exactly want to come here."

"Well that *was* quite obvious." Muriel wore a pretty tweed suit over the jumper. Pauline thought how attractive and fulfilled she looked. What a sensible woman she was never to have married, to have resisted the pressures that would doubtless have been put upon her to forsake spinsterhood. Instead she had a life and career which she had obviously found deeply satisfying, the financial rewards of which now enabled her to lead a life of leisure.

She, Pauline, would probably be tied to some kind of job for the rest of her life.

"She also has this curious obsession about the house being unhappy," Muriel went on. "I think it's preyed on her mind."

"I think so too. However," Pauline's arms felt goose-pimply, even with a warm woolly on top and a centrally heated house, and she rubbed them vigorously, "I do think there *is* something wrong with that house."

"Oh really?" Muriel looked at her with surprise.

"I mean I've only been there a couple of days. I was so looking forward to being in the country. I'm also not, as you might realize, a very imaginative person. But I don't feel comfortable in that house. It makes me uneasy. If you'd known Helen in the old days you'd be amazed at the change. She's so tense all the time. Our girls, who were *such* good friends, are always rowing. Even the cat's been behaving oddly and yesterday I noticed a very odd smell, a nasty smell that suddenly came and went."

"Oh dear!" Muriel looked concerned. "That *sounds* like drains."

"Well it was as horrible as drains, but it was a peculiar smell. Musty, very sharp. The cat also noticed it and started prowling around, but Helen, who came in a moment later, said she couldn't smell a thing. She said it was silage from outside."

"Probably." Muriel looked relieved at the logic of the explanation.

"However . . ." Pauline lowered her voice even more confidentially, "what affected Helen so badly happened afterwards." And, unable to resist sharing her burden, she told Muriel in some detail about the visit to the empty cottage and Helen's story about the cat. Concluding: "So *I* think these headaches have obviously something to do with her state of mind, don't you?"

"I find that an absolutely incredible story." Muriel's

face had turned quite ashen. "Most unsettling, and distressing for you both. I *remember* when she brought the cat back after it had been missing for ages. She told *me* about the old lady. There's no doubt at all she thought she saw her. It was very real for her."

"But the place has been empty for five years. It's practically a ruin."

"But how would Helen know about Mrs Markham? I mean she obviously existed, Helen didn't make her up."

Pauline hadn't the answer and remained silent.

"However," Muriel said briskly, recovering her composure, "she must obviously see a doctor and get checked out. That is most important, to eliminate anything serious like . . . well, a brain tumour or something."

"A brain tumour?" Pauline looked aghast.

"Well you know. Disfunctioning of the brain can create all sorts of strange and worrying delusions."

Dr Hamilton shone a torch first in one of Helen's eyes then the other, flicking back her lids and examining them closely. Then he switched off the torch and stood back.

"How long have you been having these headaches you say?"

"About six months."

"And have you got one now?"

She nodded, looking pale and weak, lying back against the pillow in her bed. In the background Pauline watched with a worried frown.

The doctor leaned forward again gingerly pressing his fingers and thumbs against the sinuses on both sides of her face. "Any pain?"

She nodded.

"It could be sinus," he went on, "or migraine, as the headaches are prolonged. Have you ever had sinusitis or migraine before?"

Helen shook her head. "I hardly ever had a headache in my life."

"Yet you were on some sort of drug when you came down here?"

"My doctor gave me tranquillizers and an anti-depressant."

"And do you know what they were?"

She shook her head.

"I see I shall have to get your case notes from your previous doctor. I take it you want to register with my practice?"

"Oh yes please." Helen nodded vigorously. "I should have done it before."

"Well anyway I'll prescribe in the meantime a strong painkiller, a mild analgesic, and wait until I hear from your doctor. I would also like to arrange for you to have a scan if the headaches don't clear up."

"Scan?" Helen looked aghast.

"Nothing serious." He smiled reassuringly at her. "It's a perfectly normal precaution and I'm sure it will show a normal result. Now," he opened his case and produced some tablets wrapped in foil, "this is an emergency supply until you can get to the chemist. I take it you have a car?"

"My husband will get them tomorrow. He works in Yeovil."

"Well . . . " the doctor looked doubtful.

"I'll ask Muriel," Pauline chipped in. "I'm sure she'll run me to the nearest chemist."

"Miss Forbes will do anything for anybody," Dr Hamilton said admiringly. "A great person to have as a neighbour. Couldn't be better."

After she had seen the doctor out Pauline went upstairs to Helen's room. Helen was just finishing the effervescent tablets the doctor had given her and which Pauline had put into a glass of water.

"Urgh!" Helen made a face and licked her lips. "It's bitter. I feel a little better though."

"That's good. Like a cup of tea?"

"Mmm." Helen leaned back against the pillow. "What did he say? Does he think I'm bonkers?"

"He didn't say anything and I don't think he does."

"You didn't tell him about—"

"Of course not," Pauline said sharply.

"You don't believe it yourself, do you?"

"I don't know what to think." Pauline sat on the side of the bed and took Helen's hand. "Honestly love, I don't. I think you're all shook up and overwrought, but I'm glad now you're in the hands of a good doctor who, I'm sure, will have you straightened out in no time."

Pauline made tea for herself and Helen and took it upstairs. She sat in a chair by the side of the bed drinking hers, while Helen seemed cheered by the tea, or maybe it was the medicine she'd just had. The colour was slowly returning to her cheeks and she seemed more relaxed, though drowsy.

"I think these pills are making me sleepy," she said putting her empty cup on the bedside table.

"Is the head any better?"

"Yes I think it is. I think I'll have a snooze and then I'll get up and make the supper."

"Don't be silly."

"No I must. John . . . hates ill health you know."

"That's just too bad about John. In fact I told John this morning he should bring something home, fish and chips, a Tandoori or a Chinese takeaway. I want you to have a jolly good rest."

"You're so good." Helen leaned her head back with a deep sigh. "I see why you're so good at your job. I just don't know what I'll do without you. I wish you could stay."

"I'll keep in touch, love." Pauline straightened the duvet over her. "But frankly I think if I stayed in the country too long I'd end up, well . . . like you."

*   *   *

110

Pauline saw Helen settled, drew the curtains to shut out the afternoon sun and, taking the tray downstairs, washed up the cups. She went into the sitting room and turned on the TV, sat down, putting her legs up on the pouffe. But the programmes on offer didn't interest her and she soon switched off. Anyway she felt restless and disinclined to settle.

She looked round for the cat and decided she hadn't seen her that day. Or had she been about in the morning? She couldn't quite remember now. The cat somehow disturbed her because it was linked to that very odd business about the house and Mrs Markham. If Skittles didn't go there – and how could she? – where did she go and where had she spent her missing weeks?

Pauline looked out of the window and a resolution formed in her mind, one that she was half afraid of yet determined all the same to carry out. She crept upstairs to make sure that Helen was asleep and then, going back to the hall, put on her quilted anorak, wound a scarf round her neck and pulled on her thick suede boots, fastening the straps at the top.

She had a final look around for the cat, opened the back door, couldn't find her and then let herself out through the front door, taking the spare set of keys which hung on a hook in the hall.

Opposite, Muriel's garage doors were open. She had very kindly taken the girls to Bournemouth after calling the doctor. Hamilton was right. She was a good, kind, sensible person to have about the place and Pauline was glad of it because she knew that as soon as she decently could she was going home. With a kind neighbour and a good doctor Helen was in capable hands and John, for all his peculiarities, his coldness, obviously cared and was worried about her. Anyway men were like that. They hated women to be ill. Helen was her friend. But not her responsibility. Besides after her stay in Tip Hollow she'd need a few days' rest to be fit for work!

111

Pauline walked briskly down the road, hands deep in her pockets, trying hard to appreciate the beauty of the countryside.

Well it *was* very beautiful, especially on a day like this; a pale wintry sunshine making the scenery, with its tall fir trees outlined against the sky, look almost Alpine. Not that she'd ever been to the Alps but one saw plenty of pictures.

She came to the bridge, crossed it and walked slowly along the village street, feeling, truthfully, rather foolhardy, a bit apprehensive. Few people were about. She came to the post office, lingered for a few moments gazing at the notices in the windows, and thought of Helen's postcard about the cat. What was the truth of that? What really could have happened?

It was a complete mystery.

She crossed the road and, feeling more fearful now, walked slowly to the cottage with the thatched roof standing by itself at the end of the road.

It only had a very small garden and this time she didn't unfasten the gate and go in, but stood there staring at it, willing herself to see a face in the window, some sign of life; willing herself to see it as Helen *thought* she had seen it that day when, everyone agreed, she had brought Skittles back home. No dispute about that.

Or had she only thought she had, and did Skittles just turn up out of the blue as so many cats did? Just appeared at the back door, like the day she jumped up on the kitchen windowsill after being missing for a couple of days?

That really looked the most likely solution. Helen had somehow imagined all this. Maybe she'd seen the cottage and something about it touched her imagination and then, not feeling well and brooding . . . Pauline shrugged. No it didn't make sense. Not Helen.

Well there was no one there now, and had not been for a very long time.

It was beginning to get dark and, she thought, much

colder. She wound her scarf more securely round her neck and, hands once more deep in her pockets, wandered back up the village street, past the post office, the row of thatched cottages (they were not at all like the one she'd just been looking at) and past the lane where the church was.

She stopped suddenly and retraced her steps, turning into the lane and up towards the church which stood at the end. It was a pretty church with a square Norman tower, and a lich-gate led into the churchyard with a row of tall cypresses on either side of the path leading to the church door.

Pauline began slightly to regret that she had come. She walked up to the door of the church, past the cypresses standing like sentinels, and was rather glad to discover, as she felt the latch, that the church was locked.

They had to do it these days, people apparently pinched the church silver, or vandals scribbled rude words on the walls.

She continued to follow the path round the church and stood looking at the tombstones that filled up the yard to the back wall. She wandered among the stones, pausing every now and again to read the legend inscribed: 'Here Lies' 'In Loving Memory' 'Sacred to the Memory of . . .' Well it came to us all. It was something that, along with a good many other people, she didn't like to think of, dwell upon: her own demise.

Out of the corner of her eye she saw a movement and her heart began to beat uncomfortably fast. A grey shadow seemed to emerge by one of the graves in the corner of the yard.

A shadow . . . a cat! She laughed nervously, putting her hand to her fluttering heart. Talking about scaring oneself to death . . . a cat . . . Skittles? She went closer and closer still.

Skittles sat at the foot of the Celtic cross which marked the grave, washing her face as though she hadn't a care

113

in the world. Paw up to cheek, over her ears, back to her mouth, lick and begin all over again.

Pauline knew that she didn't need to read the inscription on the grave, but all the same she did, bending over as Skittles, recognizing her, interrupted her toilet and came over to her with a welcoming miaow and began to rub herself against Pauline's legs.

> *'Sacred to the memory of Rita Markham*
> *Widow of Henry Markham*
> *Born . . . Died . . .'*

Yes, five years before. Five years dead.

Stooping, Pauline picked up Skittles, who settled apparently contentedly in her arms, nuzzling her face and purring with sheer contentment.

Pauline stood there for a long time, hugging the cat, her warm body so vibrant and alive, staring at the granite cross and wondering what secrets the stone could tell her, had it been able to speak.

PART II

For Richer, For Poorer

Chapter Seven

"Moonlight Express at 7–2," the man said, slipping a bundle of notes under the window of the betting shop and glancing surreptitiously over his shoulder as he did, as though he expected someone to be there watching him.

The bookie counted out the notes: Five hundred pounds in twenties, looked at the punter and gave him his slip without comment. The man left the betting shop, collar well up to hide his face, and strolled round to the large car-park in Sherborne. He drove swiftly along the A30 towards Yeovil with that familiar feeling of excitement, mingled with fear, that always possessed him when he gambled other people's money on the horses.

Helen missed Pauline terribly for days after she left prematurely, because she said the kids' rowing got on her nerves. Helen begged them to be quiet, pleaded with Pauline to stay on a bit longer, but Pauline was adamant. She said she hadn't been sleeping well and, anyway, she was worried about her mother who had been in hospital, a story Helen suspected was a fib.

So John had taken Pauline and Sharon, still in the final stage of a row with Meg, to the station and Helen, alone again, tried to come to grips with the fresh emotional turmoil that the trip to the cottage had brought about.

After Pauline left, Muriel became oddly supportive, much more so than before. She popped in nearly every day and several times offered Helen a lift to wherever she was going: Dorchester, Bournemouth, Bath, Bristol, always on the move.

Helen wanted to get away, but she also wanted to stay at home. Once she was in the house for a bit she forgot her fears; but when she had been away and came back to the house, especially if she was alone, they all seemed to gather around again threatening to overwhelm her.

January was a horrible month. Well it usually was anywhere. Most of England suffered in January. There was snow in the north, places cut off for days, and heavy storms in the south. In Dorset, which seemed to have a peculiar climate of its own, it was mild but very wet. Every day the rain poured down and at one time the main street of the village had been flooded. Much of Somerset was flooded, parts of Devon became inaccessible, and Cornwall had its first real snow for years.

Endless, miserable rain. It got on one's nerves. She turned her back to the window and, taking her coffee to the table, drew the *Daily Mail* towards her. They were lucky to have papers delivered; some small boy who needed money so badly he climbed up the hill and down again to deliver to the estate in the dark of early morning.

It was warm in the house. The kitchen was the cosiest place in it and she spent a lot of time there. Skittles, who didn't like rain and seemed to have ceased her wandering for the winter months, was curled up on her customary chair, nose to tail, fast asleep. In the background came some cheerful music from Radio One. There was a soft tap on the kitchen door and, as Helen looked up, she saw Muriel's shadow on the other side.

"Come in," she called and pushed the paper away. She felt Muriel was a bit like the care-lady who popped in every day to see you were all right, someone like Pauline. It was kind of Muriel, but it was also a bit patronizing. She could never regard her as a close friend, a buddy like Pauline.

118

"How are we today?" Muriel would say, and that was what she said now.

To which Helen replied, "Fine." She would like to have added, "I do wish to God, Muriel, you'd treat me like a normal person and not someone who was elderly, sick or disabled."

"I'm just popping into Salisbury, I wondered—"

"Not today thanks, Muriel." Helen's expression was rueful. "I think I may have one of my heads."

"Oh I'm *so* sorry." Muriel sank down on to a chair and gazed at her. "What does the doctor say?"

"Well the scan showed nothing, of course." Helen got up and plugged in the kettle, getting a mug for Muriel's coffee. "Thank heaven."

"Thank heaven," Muriel echoed.

"He thinks it's some form of migraine and has me on medication, also some pills—"

"Pills!" Muriel looked knowledgeable.

"*Very* mild tranquillizer. To calm me down."

"And do they?"

"I *think* so." Helen poured water over the coffee, added milk, and passed the mug across to Muriel. "I think they also make me feel a bit flat, depressed . . . but no more scary turns." She knew Pauline and Muriel had had a good heart-to-heart.

"Well thank goodness for that." Muriel looked cheerily around. "You know it is a very *cosy* house. I mean this kitchen is very comfy." She gazed across at Skittles. "And the cat thinks so too."

"I know you must have thought I was *barmy*—"

"Not *barmy*," Muriel said hastily. "Not at all. I just think the upheaval of the move disturbed you. You were very edgy like . . . like," she fluttered her fingers in the air searching for the right expression, "like someone on a very sharp knife edge. Now you're much calmer." She nodded approvingly and looked out of the window. "Come the spring and you'll feel a different woman."

119

She paused and seemed to be considering something. "I still think, however, that you need to get out more. Have you completely given up the idea of a part-time job?"

"Well, until I can get a car. It's a case of chicken and egg you know. No job until I can get a car, and no car until I get a job."

"You can get them so cheaply . . . practically next to nothing." Muriel again flicked her fingers in the air.

"*That's* what I tell John, but he says we have no money."

"It's none of my business, of course." Muriel put one leg over the other, thus seeming clearly to make it her business. "But I can't understand just why you *are* so hard up."

"Well there are the children," Helen bristled, implying that Muriel as an unmarried woman knew nothing about children. "They're always a drain, always wanting something. There was the move, that was *very* expensive."

"I know but John has a good job and you got the house so cheap. Besides, you always say he's so careful."

Helen got up and went over to the sink to rinse her mug. Something about the straight line of her back told Muriel that the conversation was unwelcome. She too rose.

"Well if you're sure about Salisbury . . . ?"

"Quite sure. Thank you." Helen turned and smiled politely. "And I *do* appreciate your concern, and thanks for everything."

"Nothing you want?" Muriel began to move towards the door.

"Not a thing. John is getting very good at doing the shopping and he is taking me in on Saturday for a big shop. Oh, by the way, Jake has been made Scout leader."

"Oh that's good news."

"Yes, they think very highly of him already, and *Meg* is in the school play."

"Better and better. Things'll improve, you'll see."

"Things *have* improved," Helen said firmly and, opening the door for her, ushered her out.

"Any news from Pauline?" Muriel, on her way down the path, paused and turned round. Helen shook her head.

"Such a nice person," Muriel added, then waved and Helen watched her rounding the corner until she was out of sight.

She shut the door, returned to the table and slumped into her chair. Muriel and Pauline had certainly got on. There wasn't a thing Muriel didn't know. Well you couldn't blame Pauline, who wanted to share her worry. She knew that Pauline thought she'd got the answer: that she, Helen, had seen *Skittles* in the *graveyard* and in a confused, neurotic state transferred the dead woman into the empty and deserted house. Pauline told her elatedly about how she'd seen Skittles, and had rushed back with her new theory which she thought explained everything.

At the time Helen pretended to consider the matter. It was a thought, if a tenuous one. It took her right off the hook because she knew Pauline was worried about her mental stability.

However Helen knew quite well and with certainty that she *had* visited the house, visited it twice, and that she had met with an old lady who was supposed to be long dead.

The grandfather clock in the hall chimed eleven. It had belonged to John's grandfather and was much prized by him as a family heirloom. Yet sometimes she hated the relentless, heavy ticking of the clock, the relentless passing of the hours.

She fell back to thinking about her conversation with Muriel again. And, come to that, *why* hadn't they any money? It really was none of Muriel's business, but she had a point. John had always been so careful; his only obvious extravagances were his stupid battle maps and his war books, but he seemed to have lost interest in that now that he could no longer get to war games.

In many ways, after nearly sixteen years of marriage, Helen still found her husband something of a mystery and, like many other people she knew, including Pauline and her mother, she was sometimes at a loss to explain why on earth she had ever married him. It seemed the fashion at the time; marry young and have some fun. It was a chic, fashionable thing to do. Little did she know.

Married to someone with whom she had so very little in common.

The clock finished striking the hour and she suddenly wished she had accepted Muriel's invitation to go to Salisbury. *Why* hadn't she? Truth to tell, she hadn't a headache, not the suspicion of one. Her tranquillizers calmed her, kept her on an even keel. They made her feel a bit flat, but it was better than being so keyed up all the time, as though one's perceptions were heightened to an alarming, frightening degree.

She remained staring out of the window, wondering exactly what she should do with the rest of the day. She really had time on her hands, not nearly enough to do. Stupid not to have accepted Muriel's invitation. It was so bleak, so wet outside, that was why. Also she felt lazy, apathetic; she was almost tempted to go back to bed and spend the day there.

Skittles looked up, stretched, turned round and seemed to be preparing to settle down and go back to sleep again. But instead she changed her mind and looked pointedly at the door leading from the kitchen to the hall. It was slightly ajar and Helen felt a flutter of apprehension. Had it been before? She couldn't remember.

"Skittles," she called winsomely, patting her lap, "come here."

But Skittles stayed where she was, continuing to look fixedly at the door which seemed to mesmerize her.

And then it began again, that awful feeling of crawling, something creeping over her skin, seeming to start at the nape of her neck, proceed down her back and along each leg to her toes. She could feel the hair on her arms standing on end. She followed the cat's gaze, wanting to shut the door yet also wanting to see what was happening on the other side.

She felt pulverized with fear, parched. She couldn't have cried out or moved if she tried.

And then there was the smell . . . the horrible smell that Pauline had described. It began to waft towards her like a pungent whiff of effluent that one sometimes got when passing a public lavatory where the standard of hygiene left much to be desired.

The door began slowly to swing open . . . the clock struck eleven . . . but surely it already had? Skittles started towards the door and stopped as a sudden rush of air seemed to hit her in mid-stride, the hair on her back starting to rise. Helen felt herself choking, dying . . . she grasped her throat.

Everything momentarily seemed suspended in time until the clock stopped chiming again.

Slowly the door swung back to its original position, slightly ajar. Skittles sat down in a matter-of-fact manner as though the tension had gone out of her and began a thorough wash.

Helen felt all her energy drain from her and slumped on the table, her head resting on her arms.

Moments later Skittles jumped on to her lap, purring deeply as though to try to comfort her.

But, despite her efforts, Helen remained cold and inert, convinced that some impenetrable spirit of evil resided in the house.

John Tempest leaned forward with an encouraging smile and pointed to the spot where a signature was needed.

"There, Mrs Robinson, if you'd just sign . . ."

Mrs Robinson bent over without looking at the document and signed in the place indicated, while John examined her cheque to make sure that everything was in order.

"And if you'd sign the authorization for the monthly standing order," he said pointing to another spot on the document, "I shan't trouble you any further."

"No trouble at all Mr Tempest." Mrs Robinson added her signature with a flourish. "And thank *you* very much. You've been most helpful."

"That's what we're here for Mrs Robinson." John stood up and, collecting the documents, neatly appended the cheque and placed it in his briefcase. "And if there's ever *any* problem you will get in touch with me? Personally, with me please."

Mrs Robinson smiled. He was such a nice man; so calm, *and* helpful, and such a comfort too after she'd been bereaved; someone you could talk to. It was very good to know that one could invest one's money, make it work for one with very little risk. Well none at all actually. Mr Tempest had assured her that investing in Profitable Life was like putting money in the Bank of England.

Mrs Robinson lived on a large, sprawling estate on the outskirts of Yeovil. It was much larger than the Tip Hollow estate, seemed to go on for miles, and the houses were mostly neat semis with pockets of garden front and back.

She had lived there for thirty years with Mr Robinson. Unfortunately there had been no children. It was just one of those things, but as one got older it did leave one with a feeling of emptiness, as though one hadn't got that comfort and security for the future so many other couples had. She and Tom, her husband, had felt that not having children made them close, and perhaps it did. But it also meant that when he was suddenly

124

taken from her, following a heart attack, she had no one at all.

She'd first come across Mr Tempest just before Christmas when there was all that business seeing to Tom's will and there was quite a tidy sum from his life insurance policy. Mr Tempest advised on insurance and went to the trouble of coming out to see her as she had no car and it wasn't all that convenient going into the office. He'd advised her to put a lump sum in a special account which paid a high rate of interest.

He was kindness itself. Such an *understanding* man with a family of his own. She stood at the doorway in the pale wintry sunshine waving him goodbye.

John drove away from the house on to the main road and then away from the town towards the pretty village of Montacute with its beautiful stately home, now owned by the National Trust. Once upon a time a wealthy family had inhabited Montacute but they hadn't husbanded their fortune, and in common with many others like them, lost all their money.

John used to like to drive out to Montacute, have half a pint and a sandwich in the pub there, and then gaze at the outside of the house, closed in winter, as though merely looking at it would be a lesson to him to husband his fortune, to realize what happened to those who squandered their money instead of making it work for them.

This time however he didn't go to the village but parked in a layby by the side of the road and drew out the papers that he had completed on Mrs Robinson's behalf and she had signed. Everything was in order. He looked at the cheque for a first payment of £2,500.

Then he drove all the way to Exeter to pay it into a special bank account in a town where he was unknown.

"Profitable Life," Mr Stewart said squinting at the papers

John put before him. Then he pointed to the masthead with a stubby finger. "It says here: 'ICUMEN LIFE TRUST'."

"Profitable Life is a subsidiary," John said smoothly. "Dealing with life insurance where *we* invest the funds for you. As with all forms of investment," he said, assuming a grave, schoolmasterly attitude, "funds can decrease as well as increase; but I think you will find that you will be very satisfied with your investment which, when you retire, will yield a sizeable nest egg."

Mr Stewart didn't seem too sure. He was a builder and he had already lost a lot of money. He had gone to Icumen to close his account, but the manager had asked him to step into his office and outlined the attractions of the new investment fund which the firm was pioneering.

Profitable Life, Mr Stewart thought to himself, didn't seem quite right; but there it was with the correct address, the registered office number, the VAT number and so on and so forth. Member of FIMBRA, the Insurance Brokers Registration Council – you name it, it was all there.

"Only very *select* customers are being approached," John said a little nervously, realizing his mouth was quite dry. Foolish this, to try to ensnare a new customer on the very premises. Also he should stick to widows and easily influenced women who were a soft touch. Unsuccessful businessman he might be, but Stewart obviously smelled a rat.

"Think about it," John said drawing the documents towards him out of Stewart's grasp.

"Well if you let me keep them I'll study them." Stewart tried to stop the retreating papers, but John slid them towards himself with the dexterity of a conjuror before shuffling them together and popping them into a folder, which he put into a drawer on the right hand side of his desk.

"I'm sorry but they're rather confidential," John said with a smile, getting to his feet and putting out a hand.

"Let me know if you change your mind and I'll gladly come and see you."

He saw Mr Stewart to the door of his office, shook hands, and then glanced at his watch.

There was just time to put something on the 2.30 at Lingfield.

"And how have you been Mrs Tempest?" Dr Hamilton said with a practised smile as he fastened the cuff round Helen's arm to measure her blood pressure, looking at the gauge as the mercury first shot up and then began to come down.

"Mmm," the doctor muttered noncommittally, unfastened the cuff and made a note on the patient's card.

"Is it all right doctor?" Helen asked anxiously, always with that feeling of anxiety, of dread, these days, as though at any moment, anywhere, about anything, something was bound to go wrong.

"It's a bit higher than I would have expected, but not dangerously high. Are you taking the medication?"

"Yes," she lowered her eyes, "but I don't want to get hooked. You know you read so many awful things—"

"Oh I shall keep an eye on you," he said scribbling out another prescription on his pad, tearing it off and giving it to her. "Now how have the heads been?"

"Mmm fine." She seemed uncertain and then pressed the places under her eyes. "I do think it is in the sinuses."

The doctor leaned over and applied pressure with his forefinger and thumbs.

"Are they tender now?"

"Mmm kind of."

"Well we'll try a decongestant, twice a day, twice in each nostril. Now careful you don't get too dependent on *that* because it can be habit forming."

"Oh?" Alarm again.

"All I mean is that you get used to clearing your nostrils twice a day and it affects the delicate linings,

127

the mucus membrane, so that they are unable to work for themselves."

He saw the anxiety clear from her face. Alternately she looked anxious and relieved in the space of a short interview, with bewildering rapidity.

Really she was a very highly strung woman. He made another note on his record card before sliding it into its sleeve.

"Come and see me again in about a month," he said standing up and, as he showed her to the door. "Settling down now in Tip Hollow?"

Helen shook her head. "I don't think I ever will."

"No chance of a move?"

"Not yet."

"Until then keep on taking the medicine," Dr Hamilton said with a smile as his nurse got up from the reception desk and showed Helen to the outer door.

There were no other patients. Surgery was over and the nurse locked the door after the departing Helen, while the doctor stood watching her go down the path towards the car where Muriel awaited her.

"It's strange that she's so like the last woman who lived there," he said with a puzzled frown. "Susan Becket."

"Oh her?" The nurse smiled. "She used to come here every week, at least."

"And for very much the same symptoms: nervous, depressed, anxious. Maybe it's something in the environment, something about that hill."

The nurse looked at him incredulously. "You've got to be joking," she said.

"Well, you read about it all the time; environmental pollution. There's something in it you know."

"Oh I know that, but in that case everyone on that hill would be coming to see you."

"True," Dr Hamilton acknowledged, and turned into his consulting room, putting the matter out of his mind.

*   *   *

128

"Everything OK?" Muriel looked enquiringly at Helen as she closed the gate of the garden leading to the doctor's surgery.

"He says my blood pressure's a bit up, but not to worry," she said slipping into the seat beside her. "Just keep on taking the tablets."

"And do you?" Muriel put the car into gear.

"Occasionally. Every now and then."

"Shouldn't you take them regularly?"

"I don't want to get *hooked*. You read such awful things."

"Oh but I'm sure—"

"Well that's how I feel." A stubborn note entered Helen's voice. "You know doctors don't really care."

"Oh but Doctor Hamilton—"

"Is just like all the rest," Helen said shortly. "Do you mind dropping me off at the village Muriel? There's something I want to do."

They were approaching Tip Hollow from the village two miles away where the doctor's surgery was. Muriel slowed down to dip into Tip Hollow from the escarpment from which they could see the estate at the top of the hill on the other side. It all looked very peaceful, very picturesque.

"Soon be spring," Muriel indicated the burgeoning vegetation on either side. "It's the most beautiful time of the year here."

Helen, preoccupied, nodded, looking neither to right nor left but straight on.

"You'll have to be doing something about your garden." Muriel braked as they went down the hill. "Maybe get a man in."

"Huh!" Helen snorted. "The only man I'll be getting in is my husband. He wouldn't pay a penny for a gardener."

"A good digging over and some fine topsoil with plenty of fertilizer."

Truth to tell, Muriel thought, the garden opposite her was a disgrace and reflected on all the people who lived on the estate, whose neat, well kept gardens added to the attraction and, more importantly, the price.

She often asked herself why exactly she had come to live at Tip Hollow, such an out of the way place with no one she knew for miles. Then there was the unfortunate business of having the Beckets, and now the Tempests, families full of problems. Well families frequently did; it was only those sensible enough to remain single who avoided them.

"If you put me off at the post office that will be OK." Helen began to unfasten her seat belt.

"I'll wait for you."

"No really I . . ." Helen turned to her with a strained smile, "I'd rather walk."

"No but seriously—"

"To get some fresh air," Helen said, that stubborn expression returning. "Do me good."

"Fine. OK." Muriel stopped outside the post office and watched Helen get out of the car, close the door firmly and lean towards her to wave goodbye.

"Bye," Muriel called and continued along the street, across the bridge and up the hill.

Helen watched her until the car was out of sight. Then, ignoring the entrance to the post office, she walked along the road in the direction she had just come, crossed the road and walked, with measured steps, until she came to Mrs Markham's cottage. She stood on the pavement for some time gazing at it.

It looked more derelict than ever, paint peeling from the outside walls, from the woodwork round the door and windows, the panes deeply encrusted with grime. She stared hard at the cottage willing somehow to turn back time so that the door would open and the old lady would invite her in. She once read about two very sensible-minded English schoolmistresses who claimed that they had gone back to the Court of Versailles and Louis XIV.

She closed her eyes and tried very hard, willing with all her mind, her strength, her heart. She could see the old lady and the fire burning in the hearth, the shining polished furniture, some of it obviously valuable, the profusion of country flowers. She could smell them, a beautiful all-pervasive fragrance, and see the twinkling eyes of the dear old lady. She could recall every word of their conversation. Was *this* a delusion? And then in a corner curled up on a chair was Skittles, curiously contented and obviously at home, reluctant to be taken back to the house at the top of the hill.

Helen hesitated to open her eyes because she half wanted, yet half dreaded, that when she did she would see the house as it had been when she visited it six months before. What would she do if she opened her eyes and saw the windows sparkling, the door opening and Mrs Markham's white head peep round the door? Would she go in? Would she know she was entering another world, one peopled by the dead . . .

She breathed deeply, she felt herself sway and clutched the gate for support at the same time as she opened her eyes: the house was as it had been, long empty, deserted.

Helen steadied herself against the gate shaking her head with relief, yet also aware of a keen sense of disappointment.

She was not mad – now. Had she been? Had she been suffering from an intense delusion from the time she walked into the house until she walked out of it again with Skittles safely in the basket? She knew everyone else thought she was deluded, even Pauline; certainly not *mad*, but suffering from disorientation and stress.

Yet did she herself believe in the theories of time as the two schoolteachers who had walked from the 19th century into the 17th century French Court?

She turned away and walked back along the street, crossing the road, past the post office, until she reached Church Lane. At the end the church seemed to beckon. She had never visited Mrs Markham's grave, never dared. Something had held her back, but today she felt stronger. The lane looked so pretty in its spring foliage, the church inviting. There was a gentle breeze in the air and the sun had come out. She paused by the lich-gate, opened it and went into the churchyard. She had no idea where the grave was, and she didn't want to know. She didn't want to see the words engraved in stone, know for a fact that the decayed bones of that warm, kindly, smiling woman lay there.

Instead she turned to the church. Finding the door open she went inside and, flinging herself on one of the kneelers beautifully embroidered by the women of the parish, raised her eyes towards the cross hanging above the altar; the pitiful, sad, desolate face of the suffering Christ. She bent her head in prayer for the soul of Mrs Markham, for the souls of all those buried in Tip Hollow, for all the people who lived there, and for herself.

Helen came out of the church feeling strangely calm and at peace. She was not religious, had not been in a church since Meg was christened. But she was not strictly speaking a non-believer, although she hadn't prayed for years. Big occasions moved her however; national ceremonies, war anniversaries, that kind of thing, and when the nation went to St Paul's or Westminster Abbey she went there in spirit via the TV set, eyes moistening slightly, a lump rising in the throat as the great religious melodramas unfolded.

Outside the church she stood in the yard looking about

her, keenly aware of the filigree tracery of the leaves, the dappled sunshine on the old stone graves.

She opened the gate and walked along the lane, left at the end until she came to the bridge and, crossing it, she began to follow the winding lane to the top.

As she came in sight of the houses the clear blue sky grew overcast and she felt a drop or two of rain on her face. April, a time of quick changes from sunshine to showers and back again. She hurried towards the house aware of the very black cloud that hovered over it, eager to get indoors before it burst.

Suddenly before her astonished eyes the house extended outward growing to such enormous dimensions, like a huge pumpkin, that she thought it would burst . . . bigger, bigger and bigger it grew as she watched with dismayed stupefaction, hand to her mouth, too frightened even to scream.

Then just as suddenly it contracted again, grew alarmingly thin and seemed to shoot up like a crazy animation on the TV screen. The sky overhead grew blacker, the cloud thicker, denser, until it entirely obscured the elongated house. Then it became quite black and the whole air seemed rent asunder by terrifying sounds until, at last, she felt herself falling, pitching head first into blackness.

Muriel thought to herself, oh hell, it's going to rain. One moment the sun had been bright and hot, the next moment it had clouded over. She had taken a risk and put some clothes out on the line because she so liked drying clothes in the fresh air.

She hurried out of doors and felt a few drops of rain, looked at the sky and saw it was clearing, waited a few seconds wondering what to do. Then she saw Helen come up the lane and turn towards her house and she stood silently where she was, hoping her presence would go unnoticed, not wanting really to get into conversation with her again.

She was a little miffed at being dismissed in the village so abruptly as if she had done her job, served her purpose, and that was that. In a sense she had, but there was something about Helen's attitude that annoyed her, made her feel she was being taken for granted. There was not even an invitation for a cup of coffee, nor, she seemed to recall, a word of thanks unless a wave of the hand could be called 'thanks'.

After all it had been very *good* of her to give up half her morning taking Helen to the doctor's when there were so many other things she could be doing with her time. She had loads of letters to write, some dried flowers to press, a report to be done for the local Historical Society of which she was chairperson.

Now the moment of danger had passed. Helen had not seen her and Muriel went inside going straight to the front room to turn on the one o'clock news on the TV.

Out of her front window she saw Helen enter her gate, go up the garden path and then stop abruptly. She was staring hard at her house as if seeing something unexpected, and Muriel too stared but could see nothing untoward. But Helen remained where she was. Then she put her hand to her mouth and fell forwards on to her face just as the sun came out and the air filled with light.

Muriel ran out of the sitting room, through the front door, and was by Helen's side almost as soon as she had fallen. The woman lay prone on her face, eyes closed. Muriel's own heart beating frantically, she placed a finger against the jugular in Helen's neck and was thankful to find a strong pulse. She thought she had better leave her where she was, after, of course, making her comfortable, and was about to go back to her house to fetch a blanket and pillow before ringing the doctor when Helen's eyes fluttered and then opened and she stared incomprehensibly in front of her.

"Oh thank God you're all right," Muriel said, gazing down at her.

Helen lay there for a second and then got groggily to an upright position, upon which she turned and stared at the house. It looked quite normal; four square, and in the porch sat Skittles washing her fur. Helen looked at the house and up at Muriel.

"Anything wrong?" Muriel asked, stooping to take her arm. "I mean obviously there is something wrong, but you were staring so hard at the house."

Helen shook her head, saying nothing and, gripping Muriel's hand hard, got to her feet.

"I was going to ring the doctor—"

"Oh please don't. I think he thinks I'm a neurotic fool anyway."

"But you fainted. You didn't trip, or catch your foot. You fainted clean away," Muriel said tucking her arm through her neighbour's and leading her into the house. "I think you're a sick woman, Helen, I really do. I don't know if it's physical, mental or emotional, but I am quite sure there is something wrong with you and you must get help."

By now they were in the kitchen, Skittles skipping in front of them anxious for her bowl to be restocked with food. While they ignored her she went back and forwards, tail waving hard with displeasure. But as that display had no effect she ostentatiously licked the tiny remnants of food in the dish as if to demonstrate just how badly treated she felt herself to be.

Muriel sat Helen down at the table and put the kettle on. She made two strong mugs of tea and brought them over. Helen remained staring at the table with a frown on her face that was not so much one of puzzlement as bewilderment.

"I simply can't understand what happened," she said

135

taking the mug that Muriel held out to her. "I was feeling quite happy, quite at ease, and then . . ."

"Then?" Muriel encouraged her.

"It's this house," Helen said. "There's something terribly wrong with it."

Chapter Eight

The man in the estate agents was helpful but puzzled. "You want to know something about *Fourteen* Tip Hollow Hill, Miss Forbes?" He seemed undecided about whether or not it would be ethical to divulge information about another property.

It so happened that the agents who Muriel bought the house through and the agents for the sale of the house opposite were the same: Black, Carr and Son of Yeovil. In fact they had been the agents for the original estate when it was built in the mid-Sixties.

Muriel felt awkward. She was doing something she wouldn't normally do, would never have dreamt of doing: interfering in the affairs of someone else without their consent. But she was curious, puzzled. More than that she was worried.

She was worried about the health of Helen Tempest and it occurred to her that as the similarity between the Beckets and the present occupants was rather striking, it might be interesting to see if anyone else living there had been affected too.

"The normal thing," the young man, whose name was Douglas Jennings, said, "would be to see the deeds of the house."

"Well as they belong to the current occupiers or are lodged in the bank it's something I couldn't possibly do," Muriel said. "This is for purposes of historical research." She leaned forward confidentially. "I don't want the Tempests to think I'm being nosy."

"I don't really think we can help Miss Forbes." Mr Jennings looked up gratefully as an older man appeared and hovered as though to see if there was any way in which he could help his struggling assistant.

"It's Miss Forbes isn't it?" the man said genially. "I think I sold you your house . . ."

"Oh of course." Muriel looked up, also relieved. "It's Mr Carr isn't it?" They shook hands.

"Don't say you're selling your property already, Miss Forbes?"

"Well not just now, but I am thinking of it." Muriel surprised herself by her own admission, realizing that for some time the possibility had been latent at the back of her mind.

"Oh really?" Mr Carr gave Douglas Jennings a meaningful glance and the young man got up and offered his seat to his boss. "We'd be very pleased to handle the sale for you."

"Well I'm still thinking. But it is a very *isolated* spot."

"It is a bit out of the way," Mr Carr agreed. "However I don't think we'd have much difficulty disposing of your house when the time is right. Perhaps you wish to move nearer the town, Miss Forbes?"

"Nearer the sea I think." Muriel realized that she was getting deeper and deeper into making an admission of a half-conscious wish. "But not for a while. My interest is in the house of the people who live directly opposite me."

"Oh!" Mr Carr pursed his mouth. "I'm afraid we can't release details."

"I know that. The fact is," she paused and wriggled awkwardly in her seat. "Of course *I* don't believe in ghosts or psychic manifestations, but my neighbour who, I would have thought, was a very sane, well-balanced woman, has not been at all happy since she's been there."

Mr Carr's expression was one of polite scepticism. "What exactly do you mean, ghosts or psychic manifestations?" he asked peering at a file which Jennings had put before him. "No one ever suggested it was haunted."

"I didn't say it was haunted . . ."

"You mentioned ghosts."

"I said I didn't believe in them."

"Neither do I."

"*But* Mrs Tempest finds living in the house disturbing. She's become, frankly, slightly unhinged because of this and she's not what I'd call a neurotic woman."

"Perhaps there are other reasons." Mr Carr looked puzzled, leafing through his file which obviously pertained to Fourteen Tip Hollow Hill. "I do see, however, the property has been sold five or six times since it was built . . . which is quite a lot." He looked up at her. "It appears never to have been what you call a lucky house . . . *perhaps* an unhappy house. I mean, some people have lived quite happily on that estate for years, but number fourteen has changed hands quite often. It doesn't mean it's haunted."

He laughed good humouredly at the preposterous nature of such an idea. "I mean you are implying something of that kind, aren't you? Really, Miss Forbes, a *modern* house built of bricks and breeze blocks . . . not very likely is it? Now if you were talking about an *old* house, an eighteenth century cottage or a rectory, I might be prepared to listen, although do you know," he leaned across the desk as though anxious to impart an interesting item of information, "in all my time in the estate agency business in these parts, I have *never ever* come across a case of a house thought to be subject to any form of psychic manifestation. I suggest you consult the Land Registry if you want to pursue your research further."

He looked at his watch, got up and put out his hand. "Do let us know if you decide to move. Nothing to do

139

with your neighbour, I trust? I mean they're not annoying you or anything are they?"

"Oh no. Not at all." Muriel got up too realizing he had made her feel foolish. "I simply worry . . . you know, when people are unhappy."

"I should think it's the change from town to country." Mr Carr walked slowly with Muriel across the showroom towards the door. "A lot of people come to the country to get away and then decide it's not their cup of tea at all. Now that *is* very common. You would be surprised at the number of people who sell up after a few years and go back to the Metropolis. Now that *is* a haunting if you like. They're haunted by the memory of the excitement of city life, the noise and the smells. Sometimes I think it's like a drug."

Muriel did a bit of shopping in the precinct at Yeovil, popped into Boots on her way to the car-park, and drove out of the town feeling rather irritated with herself, ill at ease.

She felt she had made a fool of herself going to the estate agents, and had also labelled herself in their eyes as something of a nosy parker, someone who couldn't mind her own business. She felt herself flush at the very idea. "Historian indeed," they would say, with some justification.

Nevertheless, she thought, as half-way up the hill out of the town she turned right towards Tip Hollow village, she had learned one small item of interest: even the prosaic Mr Carr had admitted it seemed never to have been a very happy house. Odd phrase for an estate agent to use!

It was true, Muriel thought, that in all her years of doing historical research and delving in the past she had never really come in contact with what one might call psychic manifestations. Some people had more imagination than others – some had none at all – and there were people who were definitely neurotic or

140

hysterical who thought they saw or heard things others didn't. After all the psychiatric wards of hospitals were full of such people.

But Helen? You would never in a thousand years have called Helen either hysterical or neurotic. That is, the Helen she first knew, when she came to the house nearly a year before.

That was why the brain tumour theory, though horrible, had been so useful as a possible physical explanation of a change in personality. How, why, no one knew, but, frankly, Helen was a nervous wreck and in a way she had affected Muriel, who had grown quite jumpy on her account, never knowing exactly what to expect.

As if to confirm her fears, as she crossed over the bridge and went up the hill, she heard the sound of an ambulance and, as she got to the top there outside the Tempest house, naturally, stood a large white van with flashing lights, the doors opening and two men emerging and running up the path.

In front of the house was a cycle, its wheels still spinning round.

After she stopped the car Muriel ran across the road and up the path to number fourteen, the door of which was open.

In the hall lay Jake, white as a sheet, with the ambulance men bending over him. At his head crouched his mother and, nearby, looking very interested in the proceedings, sat Skittles. The cat even seemed to smile, her almond eyes half closed as she looked towards Muriel in greeting.

"Whatever . . . ?" Muriel began when Jake cried out as the result of something one of the ambulance men had done to him.

"Jake fell off his bicycle." Helen got up and ran over to Muriel as soon as she saw her in the doorway. "Just outside the house." She turned pointing to the cat. "Skittles ran straight across the path as he was

141

cycling down the hill . . . probably after a mouse or something."

"You can't blame Skittles," Jake mumbled, his mouth clenched, clearly in pain.

"Of *course* you can't, darling." Still Helen gazed wrathfully at the cat. "She doesn't even seem to be particularly sorry about it."

"Nothing to be sorry about," Jake said. "I should have looked where I was going. Yeeowww!" He gave a cry of pain again.

"I think the femur is definitely broken." The ambulance man looked around at Helen. "Looks like a compound fracture." He looked severely at Jake. "You were very lucky it wasn't your head young man, not wearing a helmet."

"Oh don't *say* that." Helen put her hands to her flaming cheeks, her face clearly panic-stricken.

"Better not to think about what might have happened." Muriel put a comforting arm round her shoulders. "Don't worry. Jake will be as right as rain."

"We'll take him right away to hospital." The ambulance man stood up and, taking a notebook out of his pocket, began making notes. "They'll X-ray him. Maybe keep him in a few days, but it will be several weeks before he will be able to ride his bike again, by which time I hope he does get a safety helmet."

"May I come with you to the hospital?" Helen said.

"Of course, madam. Now, the name of the young man is . . ."

Once the details were completed, and they were brief because Jake was clearly in pain, he was put on to a stretcher and taken into the ambulance while Helen got her coat.

"Don't worry, I'll tidy up." Muriel put a hand on her arm. "Of course you've told John?"

"No I'll phone him from the hospital. He can bring me back. But oh, *Meg* will be home . . ."

142

"Why was Jake home today?" Muriel looked at her curiously.

"He was studying for his exams. He did work hard all day too then, just after lunch, he decided he'd get a breath of fresh air, and got out his bike. Of course I always consider it so *safe* up here. Just my luck."

"Accidents do happen." Muriel said, trying to sound sensible.

"But with us they happen all the time."

"You exaggerate." Muriel squeezed her arm then, spontaneously, she gave her a swift peck on the cheek. "Now you go to the hospital and leave everything to me. Don't worry about a thing. I'll see Meg has her tea. Is there anything I can do for dinner tonight?"

"I don't know how long I'll be." Helen peered anxiously at the ambulance. "I mean John will come to the hospital. Don't they set the leg under anaesthetic? We'll want to be there—"

"Don't *worry* I'll see to it all." Muriel, feeling important and useful, gave her a friendly push towards the door. "Now off you go and *don't* worry. He is so young, and accidents do happen . . . to us all, not just you."

But a lot of accidents did happen to the Tempests, Muriel thought as she stood at the window watching the ambulance, its siren sounding, disappear swiftly down the hill. There was something so horrible and heart-rending about the sound of a siren. It struck fear into one's heart just to hear it.

The sense of self-importance vanished, and she felt curiously bleak and empty as the wail of the siren grew more and more distant until, finally, it ceased altogether. Then there was stillness. It seemed terribly still.

Suddenly something rubbed itself against her leg and she jumped a foot in the air.

"Oh!" She looked down and Skittles stood there grinning up at her.

143

"*Skittles!*" she said bending down to stroke the sleek head. "You're a bundle of mischief aren't you? The *trouble* you've caused."

She sat down and the cat, who had never appeared particularly friendly towards her, jumped eagerly on her lap.

"Yes, you've caused a *lot* of trouble," she admonished, gazing searchingly into her eyes as though wishing she could speak. "First you got lost. Then . . ." Well what was the truth of that odd tale about the cottage? Hard not to agree with Pauline's theory that Helen had found the cat on the gravestone and somehow had confused . . . but it was still *odd*. Very odd. Worrying. Slightly unnerving . . .

Skittles raised her nostrils and Muriel was simultaneously aware of a peculiar smell that seemed to surround them, wafting towards them from the kitchen.

"Skittles have you let off?" she asked. But the cat's manner had changed to one of alertness, as if she sensed danger and, jumping off Muriel's lap, she stalked towards the kitchen door which was ajar, nose in the air.

Muriel, who had felt more and more apprehensive ever since the ambulance left, leaving her quite alone in the house, was aware that she felt real fear, a crawling of the skin . . . at the attitude of the cat, the menace of the half open door, at the strong, disgusting and all-pervasive smell. She tried to get up but couldn't as if anchored to the spot.

She was petrified. Petrified with fear. She thought of the dead, petrified cat in the shed and the awful feeling of impotence petrification gave you: turned to stone, to harden, deaden, stiffen. The cat had been quite stiff, its pathetic fur coat covered with years of dust, its eyes empty sockets. She shook herself and tried again to lever herself up with her hands on the arms of the chair. It was like one of those nightmares where you were pursued by something, wanted to move yet could not.

She closed her eyes and tried to take a firm grip on herself before opening them again.

Drains. That was the smell. Pauline had smelt it too. It had a perfectly rational, logical explanation. It would, also, maybe be the explanation she had been searching for, of mental depression the house seemd to bring: the headaches, Helen's nervous turns. They should get a sanitary inspector in and have the drains properly looked at. She might have known there was a sensible, practical explanation.

With a huge sense of relief she gave a sudden heave and got herself out of the chair and, simultaneously, the door to the kitchen snapped shut and she realized she was trembling.

"Anyone there?" called the voice and the door swung open again. Meg stood on the threshold swinging her school bag, looking surprised when she saw Muriel. "Where's Mum?"

"Oh it's you," Muriel said, relief flooding back again, and at the same time noticing that the dreadful smell had quite disappeared. "How long have you been here?"

"Couple of seconds. I came in the back way."

"Look," Muriel went over to her and gently took hold of her arm, "there is *nothing* to worry about, nothing. He is quite all right." She realized she was babbling as Meg looked more and more confused, and drew Meg to the sofa where she sat down beside her. "It's your brother. Jake had an accident." The words all rolled into one. "He fell off his bike. He is quite *OK* but he has gone to hospital and your mum is with him."

Then the torrent of words finished.

"But why has he gone to hospital?" Meg screwed up her face anticipating the worst.

"Because he broke his leg."

"Oh!" Meg began to wail. "You didn't say."

"You didn't give me the chance."

"You *said* he was quite all right."

"I meant that, well, he isn't dead or seriously injured. Just a clean break. He will be quite OK in no time."

"But how . . . ?" Meg flung her satchel on the floor. "Jake is very good on his bike. Very safe."

"The cat streaked out in front of him."

"The cat? Our cat?"

"Skittles, chasing a mouse or something."

"Oh she's *naughty*." Meg jumped up looking for the animal.

"No use punishing her. It's not her fault."

"But," Meg turned round, "I saw her in the woods as I was coming up the road. The school bus puts me off at the bottom by the bridge. She looked to me as though she was after a mouse then. She took no notice of me."

"But," Muriel paused, "she's in the kitchen. She was on my lap a minute or two ago. She slipped past you as you came to the door."

They both looked at each other and went into the kitchen to investigate. No sign of Skittles.

"Not here, you see," Meg said. "The back door was locked. I have a key. It was definitely Skittles on the path to the woods. You'd think I'd know my own cat. She's mine you know."

"Maybe it was a cat like her? There are several tabbies about aren't there?"

"There's only one Skittles," Meg said firmly. "Is it OK if I telephone the hospital?"

"Of course." Muriel shook herself determined to put this latest mysterious occurrence out of her mind. Hysteria was catching. Whole groups of people went down with it. Yet the cat couldn't be in two places at once, couldn't get out of locked doors, open windows.

Too obviously she was being affected by Helen and this house. Now she felt she wanted to be out of it quickly.

"Yes why don't you phone the hospital and then

come over and have tea with me? They may not be back until late."

Once back in her own safe, snug home normality returned. On the way from the Tempest house to hers she looked all around, but there was no sight of the cat. Yet she knew the cat had been on her lap. it was Skittles, and it was Meg who must have been mistaken. After all, from a distance one tabby looked fairly much like another.

Meg seemed reassured by what she heard at the hospital, excited even by the accident to her brother.

"I hope it won't effect his exams," she said with a thrill in her voice as she bit into a large slice of cake.

"Oh it won't affect his exams. He'll only be in hospital a day or two."

"They say a week. It's a very bad break."

"Oh I'm sorry; but once he's home he'll be able to revise."

"*If* he can settle down with Mum." Meg gave her a wry look. Muriel had always thought her old for her years. She was a very self-composed young lady, clever, and with an air of detachment as though she viewed the world through an old pair of eyes.

"Oh?" Muriel looked at her seeking enlightenment. They were sitting on either side of an occasional table on which Muriel had set the tea things. Muriel had cut sandwiches, and she always had a fruit cake in a tin.

"Mummy's very *strange* these days," Meg said with an air of resignation. "Not at all like she used to be."

"Really? Strange . . . how?" Trying not to be nosy, interested, encouraging the confidence of the child, maybe to help her?

"I can't really say." Meg put the teacup to her lips and drank thirstily. Then, "She's so on edge all the time. Never used to be . . ."

"Not in Worcester Park?" Muriel prompted.

147

"Oh no. Mum was like a rock. Here she's all wobbly, like jelly."

"When did it start?"

"Soon after we came. Fact is Mum didn't want to come down here."

"And you . . . and Jake?"

"We both like it. But we've a lot to do and Mum hasn't. It gets on her nerves."

"Did you talk to your father about it?"

"I can't talk to my father about anything much. I mean, if you start to get serious he doesn't want to know."

"And was *he* always like that?"

"Oh yes." Meg was very prosaic.

"Have another piece of cake." Muriel passed the plate across to her young companion whom she was beginning to find distinctly engaging. A personality. After all she had never really got to know either of the children at all.

"Thanks."

"So you could talk to Mummy, but not to Daddy?"

"I can still talk to Mummy; but I worry about her." Meg's face grew rather solemn. "I really do. There's a girl at school whose mum has had a nervous breakdown." She stared at her cake and then put it back on her plate as though her appetite had gone.

When she looked up at Muriel her eyes had all the vulnerability of a young girl who somehow felt her life was losing its moorings.

"Sometimes I'm terrified that something like that is happening to Mummy."

Muriel sat watching Meg's expressive features registering emotion of every kind – fear, anger, but above all something akin to despair. It was easy to see what Helen must have been like when young, because Meg was almost her exact youthful counterpart. It was easy to see in Meg the practical, good-natured woman that

148

Helen must have been before; marriage, childbearing, the mundane chores of daily life, but above all the move to the country, had taken their toll.

But didn't it happen to us all? Didn't we all have to grow up and lose our illusions? Those who had children sometimes wished they hadn't. Those who had none wished they had. The single envied the married, the married the single. For everyone the grass was a little greener over the other side of the fence.

Yet it was very sad, rather unnerving, to see someone so young – Meg was still only twelve – appear to lose her illusions so quickly, to be so adult in her attitude.

She came over to the chair where the young girl was sitting and crouched by her side.

"Would you like to go to the hospital tonight dear? I'll drive you."

"Better see what Dad says," Meg said anxiously, and Muriel realized that, after all, when it came to important things it was Father who called the tune.

After tea Meg called the hospital and spoke to her father, who told her that Jake was in the theatre having his leg set, that there was no need to worry, but he and her mother would stay at the hospital until he came out. It would definitely not be a good thing for her to come and see him because he would be groggy.

Muriel then spoke to John who confirmed what he had told Meg.

"How's Helen bearing up?" Muriel asked.

"Helen's fine. Do you want a word with her?"

"Please."

When Helen came to the phone her voice sounded stronger.

"Yes he's fine," she said, palpable relief in her voice. "No complications. Jake's now in the recovery room. Thank you so much for looking after Meg."

Muriel, feeling useful and in command again, told her

it was no trouble, that she would give Meg supper and wait with her until her parents returned home.

When she put the telephone down Muriel looked at the clock and saw it was now nearly six.

"You'd better go and get your homework done and I'll have supper ready. How long will it take you?"

"An hour, an hour and a half," Meg pulled down her lower lip.

Muriel looked at the clock again. "Well I'll have it ready about seven-thirty. Do you like egg and chips?"

"Love them."

"Then it will be egg and chips, apple pie and cream."

"Lovely." Meg licked her lips.

"You'll be OK in the house alone?" Muriel opened the door with a smile to show her out.

"Why shouldn't I be OK?" Meg looked curiously at her.

"No reason, I just thought you might be lonely."

"*You* don't think there's anything wrong with the house do you?" Meg looked at her suspiciously.

"Of course I don't!" Muriel said robustly.

"Well Mummy does."

"I think that's just because she's not very happy. When she settles down and perhaps does something about the garden it will be OK." She looked disapprovingly across the road to untidy flower beds, the straggly lawn. Really, for all her protestations, Helen still hadn't touched it. Muriel thought it had something to do with the proximity of the shed as well as inertia, and a reluctance, however symbolic, to put down roots.

"The garden?" Meg screwed up her face.

"Well," Muriel gestured helplessly across the road, "look at all the other houses. They have nice, tidy gardens. Now why don't *you* do something about it?" she suggested brightly looking at the eager young face.

"I think the garden is quite OK," Meg replied casually. "It just wants a few packets of seeds and someone to

150

cut the lawn. I'll see you about seven-thirty, Miss Forbes."

"Why don't you call me Muriel?" Muriel suggested. "It's so much more friendly, and you're too old for 'aunt'. Besides it's not very fashionable is it? In my day you would never call an older person by her Christian name. That's all changed. Is Muriel all right?"

Meg, looking embarrassed, didn't answer. With a sigh Muriel watched her as she ran across the road. She knew she would probably end up by being called nothing.

Egg and chips was a very easy, rather lazy meal to prepare, leaving her with plenty of time. She had a sweet tooth and as she also had a very slim figure – food was not one of her main interests in life – she usually had a sweet of some sort in the fridge. So the apple pie had been purchased only the day before and the cream had been bought to go with it.

She knew there was something niggling away at her subconscious, irritating her, and that was the question of the cat. Even her well known resources of common sense and practicality were being eroded by what was going on in the house opposite, dramas that apparently had little effect on its youngest inhabitant.

It seemed very strange that if, as Meg had insisted, she had had to unlock the back door, she could have seen the cat in the woods about five hundred yards away. This coincided with the time she, Muriel, was about to explore the smell coming from the kitchen. Yet on her way out Muriel had checked that, as well as the locked door, all the windows were shut too.

The other thing that bothered her was that Skittles had never been friendly towards her, making a beeline away from her whenever she approached rather as if she sensed that she didn't particularly like cats, was a little nervous of them, had maybe a slight phobia. Yet she'd jumped on her lap, perfectly at ease.

151

Was it possible that there was a cat very like Skittles on the loose? And which was which?

To try to solve the mystery Muriel left her house by the back door a few minutes after Meg had gone and made her way round the front and out into the road heading for the bridge.

She walked slowly as though she were merely out for an evening stroll and, indeed, it was a lovely evening for a saunter through the woods though, being a sensible woman, she would never have walked into them by herself – certainly not in the evening and probably not at any time during the day.

It made sense to take care when you read about all those awful things in the papers: women being raped and murdered, so that even in an area like this, you couldn't be sure you were safe. No, she would skirt the wood as she always did and just see if she could spot the cat, maybe on its way to the village where she kept on making these mysterious disappearances.

Muriel realized that she was indeed being affected by what she could only regard as the increasingly chaotic lives of the people in number fourteen. Maybe it might not be too bad an idea if she really did begin to look elsewhere. She had never really settled in Tip Hollow. She had made no friends and had to drive miles to see anyone she knew, except Helen, of course, and Helen was becoming a bit of a liability: hardly a friend so much as a nursing case.

Was she being selfish? Had life on her own made her like that? Always looking after Number One. People said it did. Well as far as she was concerned it was too late to change now.

She came to the path where she thought Meg had seen the cat. It was quite a broad path and led through the wood to a field at the other side which could be seen clearly from the road. The cows had just been put out to graze by the neighbouring farmer after their winter sojourn in the farm. The spring grass was succulent and tender, but the cows had now been taken in for the night and she could see no sign of them.

It was not a dark, scary close cluster of trees that kept out the light, but a pleasant woodland. The young poplars and beeches were bursting into life and the evening sun, shining through their variegated leaves, illuminated the thick carpet of bluebells and white wild garlic whose pungent aroma filled the air.

Muriel had always lived in towns or on the edge of them, pretty towns like Cambridge, Brighton and Chichester. Yet she had always loved country holidays, and when the time came to retire she chose, perhaps unwisely, a county she didn't know, and a modern house right in the middle of nowhere.

The mating season was at its height and the birds flew to and fro in their endless search for building materials. She could half imagine the blackbirds, tits, chaffinches or any number of woodland birds looking curiously down at her as she made her way hesitantly along the path.

It was ridiculous, really. The cat could be anywhere, watching *her*. The thought of all those eyes peering at her was rather unnerving, and she realized that the sun was sinking fast and night was falling. It was time to go back and get the supper, to forget this stupid business altogether. Put it out of her mind. As she turned to retrace her steps her eyes were caught by a streak of something to the right of the path – something grey – a rabbit, perhaps . . . a low flying bird?

She stood and stared, mesmerized, as a dying, last shaft of light illuminated a grey tabby cat sitting in the middle of the path calmly washing itself. One minute it hadn't been there, and then it was.

"Skittles," she called nervously bending low and flicking her fingers gently, "Skittles."

The cat took no notice of her, twitching first one ear

and then the next. That over it turned its attention to its chest with long strokes of its tongue.

Somehow it seemed vital at this point to establish the cat's identity and Muriel went nearer, almost tiptoeing, with that caressing, calming little flutter of the fingers. "Skittles," she called softly. "Skittles."

She was within a few feet of the cat when it suddenly paused in its toilet, stared at her and then, totally unexpectedly, bared its pointed teeth in a ferocious hiss and dived out of sight through the undergrowth to, she supposed, the far side of the wood.

She stood where she was feeling unnerved, shocked by something evil, malevolent she had glimpsed in those yellow eyes; eyes that evoked all the primitive savagery of its forebear in the jungle . . . the tiger.

Chapter Nine

Alan King was fiftyish, rather plump and self-satisfied, one of those people to whom life would appear to have been kind.

All of his adult years were spent with Icumen Life, which he had joined, as John Tempest was to do later on, as a young man straight from school.

Little was known of Alan King's life by his staff except that Mrs King, whose Christian name was Stella, was a comfortable, happy body, also on the plump side like her husband. She had apparently never nursed a desire to work, and was quite content to look after her husband and their two teenage boys who went to the local comprehensive school.

Sometimes Alan brought his wife to office parties, but other times he came with his secretary, with whom he was long thought, without any positive evidence, to be having an affair. Maybe this dichotomy of his domestic life was what made Alan King such a seemingly happy and contented man.

King, however, did have a dark side. He was an office bully and, in varying degrees, his staff were either frightened or terrified of him.

John Tempest had long been a protégé of Alan King, for whom he had worked in a junior position when he had first joined the company. Except that Alan was the boss, and John an underling, in many ways the two men had similar temperaments; they were considered calm, unflustered, good at their jobs, and dull. They were meticulous, well organized and clever with figures. Each could run rapidly through a column and calculate the total in a matter of seconds without the aid of a calculator. They would work out percentages and make a pretty rough guess about the value of an insurance policy without reading the small print.

The families had seldom socialized. Once a year they were invited to each other's houses for dinner when the wives made elaborate efforts with the food, although Helen tried harder than Stella because her husband had that bit further to go. It was very important to impress the boss, the man at the top. John had impressed Alan King and fawned upon him, so that he was now area manager with his own branch; a place near the top.

Alan sat now at John's desk completing his inspection of the books. Really he knew that John was so good, and the results so far had been more than satisfactory, that it hadn't been necessary to make more than a cursory inspection.

John sat watching him, a thin film of perspiration gleaming on his well-shaven top lip, his tongue darting in and out occasionally to moisten his mouth. But as Alan King turned the ledgers with patient imperturbability, he seldom looked at his protégé who sat closely watching every move he made.

Every now and then Alan paused to ask some question, check some matter of detail, and John would send for one of the clerks in the outer office who would provide the answer if he didn't know it himself.

Naturally any inspection was a nerve-racking business, but this one for John was particularly traumatic for it was the very first time in his life he had stepped out of line and hatched an elaborate and, he felt, foolproof scheme to embezzle large sums of money from the company he had served so well and faithfully for years.

But it would never have occurred to Alan King to

question his subordinate's integrity, and by the end of the day he pronounced himself satisfied with the inspection and warmly congratulated John on his management of the new branch office.

At five it was time for the staff to depart, and Alan went into the outer office to say goodbye to each one individually and thank them patronizingly for all the effort they had put into opening the new branch.

Finally the last one left and John closed and locked the door, switching out the light as he made his way back into the inner sanctum where Alan was lighting a cigarette. He offered one to John who declined in case his hand shook. He hadn't realized it would be so bad, but the afternoon had been an ordeal. After that he hoped it could only get easier as he became more practised in the art of deceit.

"A nice bunch you have here," Alan said gathering his things together and putting them into his briefcase.

"I think so."

"Not an easy job welding together a new team."

"No," John agreed, though it had helped in his deceit as no one knew him or his habits, or that it was unusual for a branch manager to spend so much time out of the office, getting new business he told them. Some new business he did, of course, put in the company, but others he kept.

"Now look are you sure I can't take you and Helen out to dinner?"

"Not at all," John protested vigorously. "She's got it all ready. We're looking forward to seeing you."

"And I'm looking forward to seeing her and the new house. Well not so new now."

"No," John said. In a way he was dreading the night as much as he had dreaded the day. Alan King for dinner and then to stay. He had had no option but to offer his boss hospitality, but by this time tomorrow he would be safely back in London.

Alan gazed appreciatively out of the window as John drove him the few miles to Tip Hollow.

"Beautiful scenery."

"Beautiful," John agreed, taking the turning off the main road.

"Sometimes I envy you, though Richmond is nice."

"Richmond's lovely." John nodded, his eye on the rear view mirror. "I think you have the best there of town and country."

"Any regrets?" Alan looked at him sharply.

"Oh no, this is a fine place to be," John said stoutly, "and the children are very happy and doing well at school."

"How's the boy's leg?"

"Mending nicely. You'll see him tonight, though Meg is spending the night with a friend."

"Jake doing GCSEs?"

"He had mocks this year." John paused. "Sadly he had to miss them."

"Oh dear that is too bad. The accident I suppose?"

John nodded. "Not just the leg but he became very depressed."

"Jake?" Alan looked at his underling incredulously. "I can't see Jake depressed! He's so sports minded, so full of beans."

"Well he was." John remained tight-lipped. "I agree it seems to contradict his personality, but he just seemed to lose interest in everything. The doctors seemed to think it quite natural in the circumstances. Anyway he didn't want to work and we can't force him."

Alan looked thoughtful. "Fifteen is he? Fifteen is a tricky age. Our oldest sailed through it, but the youngest became very difficult round about that age."

"*This* is the village," John said, anxious to change

158

the subject. "Welcome to Tip Hollow, mentioned in the Domesday Book." And he slowed down so that Alan could see it.

"Very pretty." Alan nodded. "Nice old church. Traditional. Thatched cottages. Very nice." He frowned. "A bit out of the way."

"Well, we got the house so cheaply."

"Of course and that was nice for you. You must have been able to put quite a bit by."

John didn't comment as they crossed the bridge and began the ascent to the top of the hill.

"Mmm," Alan looked round with interest. "I see. Very modern. Beautiful view. I can understand you wanting to live here."

John drove to the end of the made-up road and stopped.

"This yours?" Alan looked across at Muriel's house.

"No, the one of the other side."

"Ah!" Alan turned and studied number fourteen as though critically comparing it with its neighbours. "Haven't had much time to do anything about the garden have you?" A keen gardener himself, he expected others to emulate his own high standards.

"No. We hope to get round to it this summer."

Alan shook his head. "Pity to neglect the garden. It tells you a lot about a person." He trailed off, his eyes on the front of the house. "And the outside could do with a new coat of paint."

"That too," John said hurriedly. "We decorated inside but never quite got round . . ."

The door opened and Helen appeared on the doorstep, dressed in a pretty summery floral print dress, her pallor disguised by heavy make-up.

"That Helen?" Alan asked in surprise.

"Yes, of course."

"Well she's lost weight."

"Yes she has."

"A lot."

"You know how vain women are." John gave a sickly smile. Already the prospect of the evening seemed like staring into eternity: endless.

"I wish my wife would be more vain in that case." Alan got out of the car to be greeted on the pavement by Helen with a kiss firmly on the side of the cheek. She knew that Muriel knew who they were having to dinner, and she wanted to be certain she saw how 'in' they were with the man at the top.

Alan looked at her and his hands ran very lightly down the sides of her waist.

"I couldn't believe it was you my dear. You've lost a lot of weight."

"Middle-age spread." Helen patted her behind. "You've got to get rid of it before it's too late."

Alan's hand lingered fleetingly on her buttocks as if to test out the theory, but she knew it was also something else. He had a roving eye and was susceptible to the charms of his subordinates' wives.

"And I think John's thinner too," Alan said moving away. "I don't think you feed him properly Helen. You're all starving yourselves." Alan's hearty laugh boomed along the path, though his observant eyes were darting from one side to the other, appraising not only the garden, the state of the paintwork, but also the ambience, the whole impression that number fourteen Tip Hollow Hill made to a stranger.

He stood in the doorway and paused momentarily to absorb the atmosphere of the house, to decide whether he liked it or whether it confirmed the bad impression made by the outside. What he saw was a rather nondescript hallway painted in that euphemistic shade, beloved of decorators, especially amateur ones, known as 'magnolia'. Leading from the hall was a doorway through which he entered to discover that the lounge-diner which ran the length of the house was painted in the same colour, that

160

the carpet was cheap and hastily laid, and the furniture old and rather shabby. He recognized some of the well-worn pieces from the previous house.

Altogether it was not a good impression.

At one end the table was set in as elegant a manner as Helen was capable of, given her resources. She had laid a pink tablecloth, pink napkins, elaborately fashioned, and tall glasses which seemed to indicate champagne. From the kitchen which led off the dining area came a wholesome smell and Alan rubbed his hands.

"Smells good," he said.

As he entered the room Jake had risen from a chair and, with the aid of a stick, hobbled slowly towards him.

"Hello Mr King."

"Jake." Alan seized the young man's hand, pumping it up and down. "You've been in the wars I hear."

Jake smiled self-consciously.

"An accident on your bicycle. You must be more careful."

"It wasn't his fault," Helen said defensively. "The cat ran in front of it as he was preparing to cycle down the hill. She came from nowhere."

"That explains it. A cat." The pleasant, good-natured expression on Alan's face vanished abruptly. "I can't stand cats." He looked nervously around. "It's not here now is it?"

Helen looked around her too, just as nervously. Thank heaven there was no sign of Skittles. Helen had been nervous all day, all week. She didn't like Alan King or his uppity wife and never had. She thought them sanctimonious, self-satisfied and snobbish, with little cause. Stella King was a woman devoted to good works, always at pains to point out to Helen, on the rare occasions when they met, the superiority of her way of life. She too had a husband, two children and a home to keep, and she would certainly not neglect any of them for a part-time job, or fritter her time away in the West End on her days off.

161

Stella always made her feel inadequate, which was Stella's intention. It was also obvious to Helen that what Alan most liked and appreciated about John was his toadying acceptance of everything he did.

John reappeared from the kitchen uncorking a bottle of champagne which, after spilling a lot on the floor, he proceeded to pour into the tall glasses under the critical eyes of his boss.

"Not used to this job," he said with a deprecating grin, eyeing Alan for his reaction.

"I hope you like champagne, Alan," Helen said, eyes still roving restlessly, apprehensive that Skittles might appear and ruin the evening. She would have to make sure the back door and windows were closed and kept closed or, heaven forbid, that the cat wasn't sleeping on the freshly made bed in the spare room. She'd have to go up and find out later.

"I'd prefer a whisky if you have it." Alan made a face at the champagne bottle which confirmed what John somehow instinctively knew would be Alan's reaction.

"We bought this especially for you, in your honour."

"Well that was very good of you John, but an unnecessary expense believe me. However as you've bought it I'll drink it, but I regard the stuff as overrated. Don't you?"

John mumbled something about not being used to champagne and Jake, observing from the corner to which he had retreated, the whole procedure, meant to belittle and humiliate his father, burned inwardly with mortification and anger on his behalf.

Although he had seldom met him, Jake knew Alan King to be of paramount importance in the Tempest family fortunes. He was always being quoted and deferred to: 'Alan thinks this', 'Alan says that', and was a powerful influence on the life and, indeed, well-being of the family.

He had only visited the house in Worcester Park about

once a year and on each occasion the children were paraded before the Kings like prize exhibits in the zoo and then sent off to bed; but his visits always produced in Helen a bout of nervous prostration, and this time didn't seem any exception. She had been working for days in preparation for the visit of mighty Mr King, and already there were ominous signs that, as usual, even without his wife, the knowledgeable Stella, things weren't quite going to work; his parents ill at ease, his father clumsy with the champagne bottle.

The dinner, however, was good and proceeded with no further hitches. There was smoked salmon, a nice leg of Dorset lamb with fresh greens and new potatoes, and summer pudding. Besides the champagne there was a pleasant rosé wine from the Loire to drink. Alan mellowed visibly in the course of the evening as a semblance of amiable satiety set in and at the end of the meal, while they were still at table, he asked permission to smoke.

Gladly given, naturally, an ashtray was hurriedly produced and placed in front of him, and John had one too.

"And you young man?" Shifting his bulk towards Jake Alan unintentionally belched, recovered himself, apologized and said, "I hope *you're* not smoking."

"No, Mr King, and I don't intend to."

"Very wise." King took another puff of the weed. "Very wise. But, you see, we were caught. This business about cancer, heart trouble and so on only came to light in recent years, didn't it, John?"

John nodded, anxious to agree.

"It was earlier than that Dad," Jake said. "It was in the Fifties. You should have learned your lesson then. The facts were well known."

"Oh I don't *think* it was as long ago as the Fifties." Alan looked aggrieved. "I was only a boy myself then and you?" he looked enquiringly at John.

"I was only born in the Fifties. But I think Jake is right."

"Little 'know-all' are we?" Alan said unpleasantly, narrowing his eyes threateningly in Jake's direction.

"Not at all Mr King," Jake replied politely. "It's just that we've been studying the effects of cigarette smoking in health education, and it *was* at the beginning of the Fifties that the link between smoking and lung cancer was first proven."

"Oh well," Alan waved a hand in his direction, "I bow to your *superior* knowledge, young man." His tone was sarcastic and he tipped a broad wink at John. "Still doesn't mean we're giving it up, does it John?"

John looked at his wife. "I'd like to . . ."

"I wish he would," Helen said, wishing too that the purgatorial evening would end.

"And how is *this* young man progressing at school?" Alan rather ostentatiously blew a cloud of smoke at Jake while addressing his parents, as though he weren't there.

"Well he's been off *most* of this term," Helen self-consciously studied the tablecloth, "because of his accident."

"But surely that's no reason to stay away from *school*? And what about your exams?" Now he looked gloatingly at Jake because, of course, he already knew the answer.

"I didn't sit them," Jake replied, staring him in the face.

"But isn't next year GCSEs?"

"He really wasn't *well* enough." Helen recovered her voice. "He got very depressed, didn't you Jake?"

"*Depressed*?" Alan boomed, clearly enjoying the taste of blood. "About what? A broken leg?"

"It was *quite* a complicated fracture," John said coldly pushing his spectacles firmly up his nose.

"Nothing to get depressed about at *his* age. These

164

things are meant to be overcome . . ." Alan looked set in for a pleasant evening of baiting; the sort of thing he enjoyed.

"Excuse me *please*." Jake got up abruptly from the table looking over at his mother. "Do you mind if I leave the table Mum?"

"Of course not." Helen looked anxiously at him. "Aren't you feeling very well?"

"A bit tired," Jake passed his hand across his head, then looked aggressively over at his tormentor, "*and* I'm getting bloody sick of *this*."

King waved a pudgy hand. "It's only in *your* interests, Jake. I'm speaking as a father. And you must try and pull yourself together young man. Mustn't let these things get you down, else you'll never get anywhere in life. Will he John?" King jerked his head in John's direction.

Jake looked as though he was going to threaten Alan King with his stick, thought better of it and changed his mind, stumbling out of the room without saying 'good-night'.

There was a pregnant silence while he could be heard going furiously upstairs, thumping his stick as he did.

"I'm terribly *sorry* about that Alan." John looked helplessly at Helen. "Jake's not himself."

"He's much too young to suffer from depressions." Alan was keen to twist the knife in the wound. "You shouldn't tolerate that kind of nonsense."

"We don't regard it as 'nonsense' Alan." Helen's naked hatred was momentarily unveiled. "Jake had a very painful time with his leg. He had to go back to hospital several times, and may even now have to have another operation. He thinks that might finish his sporting career. It isn't a *simple matter* of pulling yourself together at all." Helen's voice began to rise hysterically and she too got to her feet. "And now *if* you will excuse me I have the most awful headache . . . a migraine coming on I think. Could I leave you to clear away and get the coffee John?"

165

"Of course." John jumped up in consternation. "You should have said."

"Oh dear, I'm sorry," Alan mumbled, stumbling to his feet. "Do you have a lot of these?"

"Quite a lot." Helen looked at him with animosity. "I'm sorry Alan, but I made such an effort and I think it wasn't appreciated."

"You overdid it dear." John hastily took her arm to try to lead her out of the room.

"If I lie down now I might overcome it in time to get your breakfast and say goodbye tomorrow."

"Now you just look after yourself my dear Helen." Alan placed an avuncular arm on her shoulder. "Believe me it was *all* appreciated. A lovely meal. Even Stella couldn't have done better. And don't get up to see me off. It's not necessary is it John?"

"Of course not." John echoed his master's voice.

"And let me help clear these things—" Alan began.

"Really it's *not* necessary Alan." John looked distinctly strained. "Not necessary at all." As Helen left the room he hastened across to the television. "Would you like to see the nine o'clock news? I'll just pop up and see if Helen's all right."

Alan thought that was a good idea and ambled over to the TV with his cigarette in one hand and a glass in the other. There had been two bottles of the rosé wine and, despite his apparent aversion to it, he had drunk most of the fine champagne. He had also eaten vast quantities of smoked salmon, roast lamb and summer pudding.

But his over-indulgence, instead of making him content, now brought out his innate aggressiveness and he sat glowering at the TV set muttering derogatory comments about the government, the opposition, civil servants, railmen who were on strike, above all the Irish who he couldn't abide.

"They should go back to where they came from," he

said as John, sweating profusely, the dishes still on the table, staggered in with a tray of coffee.

"I'm terribly sorry about Helen," he said beginning to pour. "Black or white?"

"Do you have any more of that champagne?" Alan ignored his question and raised his glass. "It was very good."

"I'm afraid not." John pushed his spectacles as high on his sweaty nose as he could, only to find they immediately fell down again. "We don't really drink. I could offer you sherry."

"Sherry!" Alan said derisively. "No thank you. I'll have black coffee."

As John poured, Alan watched the weather forecast, critical about the accuracy of the weather woman and particularly her lack of sexual attraction. Then he zapped off the TV, but his eyes remained on the screen.

"Well that was an excellent dinner," he said, his brow clearing. Yet there remained something in his demeanour which John found threatening; the calm before the storm. He nervously stirred his coffee expecting an onslaught, which soon came.

"Helen been having these headaches for long?"

"Not really. Only since we came here."

"No history of headaches?"

"None."

"Mmm," Alan mused. "Well that would explain a few things which worry me John."

"What is that?" John's voice was hoarse.

"Well, this place for a start." Alan gestured expansively around the room. "I mean it's a bit of a tip, isn't it?"

"You mean the house?"

"I mean the house itself," Alan emphasized. "And the garden is *appalling*. I don't think you could have touched it since you came could you?"

"Well . . . there has been a lot to do."

"The garden is the first thing to do. It sets the tone—"

"The tone of what?" John looked puzzled.

"It tells what sort of people you are. Neighbours don't like this kind of thing, you know. I mean neglect of a garden. It shows the whole estate up, especially one that's on the expensive side. This is quite a classy neighbourhood and you've got a nice house here, despite the fact it was repossessed and you got a bargain. That doesn't mean you shouldn't take care of it, look after it properly. You don't have to cheapen the whole neighbourhood. What I can't understand is that you weren't like this in Worcester Park. Nice, well-kept house, nice garden. Standards seem to have fallen John." Alan stared at him critically. "Neighbours friendly are they?" he went on as John remained silent.

"Well . . . there's a nice woman across the road. Ex-schoolmistress."

"And the others. Do you know them?"

"Not really. Most of them work."

"But didn't you give a cocktail party or go out of your way to make yourself friendly?"

"Not really. You see . . ." John stumbled for words. "Helen *hasn't* been well. Not at all well ever since we came."

"What is the matter with Helen? Haven't you found out?"

"I don't know exactly," John began to stammer. "Maybe not very much. I think the doctor thinks it's nerves."

"Nerves," Alan said derisively. "*Nerves!*"

"Well the headaches . . . general apprehension . . . depression."

"The boy's depressed too."

"Yes. It gets us all down. Frankly Alan," John finished his coffee and moved his chair a fraction nearer to the great man after looking round to make sure the door was tight shut, "I *would* very much like to move from here."

168

"But you've only just *moved* here."

"I know but we don't like it. None of us do."

"Then why did you move?"

"Because it was cheap . . . but Helen never liked the house. In fact she hates it. She seems to think it's possessed."

"It's what?" Alan's tone was a cross between mockery and incredulity.

"Well, you know, sounds silly . . . but haunted."

"A *haunted* house?" Alan thrust back his head and burst out laughing. "As modern as this?"

John nodded shamefacedly. "I know it's absurd—"

"Of course it's absurd. The woman's deluded. Whatever made her think it was haunted?"

"Possessed . . ." John hurried on. "You know 'repossessed'. The fact preyed on her mind."

"People couldn't afford it, so what? Happened to a lot of people."

"Chucked out, lost their house. She imagined, somehow, their unhappiness seeped into the walls."

"I'd never have thought of Helen letting go like that."

"Well, there you are." John studied the carpet.

"Woman's problems more like. I'll get Stella to talk to her."

That would put the lid on it, John thought guiltily, and, moving his chair closer, lowering his voice even more, said, "The fact is, Alan, I would like to move, for Helen's sake and for mine. It would give us peace of mind. I'll be frank with you. Our marriage has been going through a very rocky state. Every night I come home Helen nags at me. She wants a part-time job, she wants a car."

"Then why don't you get her a car? Might solve a lot of problems."

"Frankly I can't afford it."

"You can't *afford* it!" Alan, completely sober now, faced him squarely, folding his hands across his stomach.

169

"I don't believe that. You've always been a very careful man, John. You had a good salary. Your children went to a state school. Knowing you, you'd have driven an old car if the company hadn't given you one. You have a lot of perks, free medical care, good bonuses. I can't believe you haven't saved some money over the years. I would have thought plenty. Then what about all the profit you made on the sale of your house? I can't believe you haven't a *considerable* amount stashed away by now."

"I haven't a penny," John said. "That's the truth. If I could have a rise, and we could sell this house—"

"But where has it all gone?" Alan cupped his hand theatrically behind his ear. "I can't believe what I'm hearing . . ."

"The children you know." John's voice shrank to a whisper.

"But *I've* children, and a wife who doesn't work, and I've managed to save quite a bit of money. Believe me I've a lot of investments."

"Well your salary would be much higher—"

"My salary *is* higher." Alan's tone was comfortable, reasonable. "I'm an older man, a much older man, but I simply can't see what you've been doing with your money, John. In fact I feel quite seriously disturbed about what I've discovered this evening. Helen, the boy, your financial situation. You'd better let me have a look at your accounts as soon as you can."

"My personal accounts?" John swallowed hard.

"Your personal accounts, and quite sharpish."

Jake lay in the dark with his personal stereo playing the sort of soft, soothing music he liked; not pop music or jazz. Jake wasn't trendy. He was a serious-minded boy for whom the last few months had been very difficult. He had been about to be selected for the first eleven when he broke his leg. He was an outdoor type who enjoyed scouting, and most forms of sport, but cricket meant everything to him. In the summer months he lived for it. He thought he had a chance not only of selection, but of being made captain.

Now there was a possibility he would never play cricket again. His injury had been so much worse than was at first thought, that it had left him with one leg slightly shorter than the other and he was due, when it was least inconvenient, a major operation to try to lengthen his leg. Even then, he was warned that it mightn't work.

And that oaf . . . that unspeakable fat arse expected him not to feel depressed! To pull himself together. *He* didn't have to live in this house, isolated from his friends, his sport, and other people, with a depressed mother who grew more neurotic by the hour. *He* didn't have to listen to his parents bickering every night, not just occasionally . . . bicker, bicker, bicker, it started as soon as they went to bed.

He really hated Alan King. He was a fat toad who had openly tried to humiliate his father and denigrate his mother. His great belly obscenely overlapped with the table. He had fat, blubbery lips and an obnoxious leer. How *could* his father possibly kowtow to this odious person? His mother had nearly driven herself into the ground preparing dinner for him and what praise did she get? Her anxiety, pathetic to see, had reduced her to rubber.

Jake had heard her coming up shortly after him; she'd looked into his room. "I've got a terrible head," she'd said. "I simply have to lie down. I feel so *awful* about Alan . . ."

Jake had got off the bed on which he was lying, fully clothed, and helped his mother across to hers. Then they had sat together on her bed for a while talking. Really, she admitted, her head wasn't all that bad. She'd just had quite enough of Alan King.

Then why, Jake had asked her, had they *tolerated* him?

171

Because he was Dad's boss. Dad owed everything to him. After a while he left her trying to sleep and returned to his room.

Jake heard a movement on the stairs and turned off the stereo, listening. It was after eleven and his father and the pig Alan were coming up to bed. They'd had a long talk and doubtless more to drink. He heard them whispering on the landing outside his door. Some time later, after Alan had been to the bathroom, the light went off and there was silence. Dead silence.

Jake felt that the house was full of menace. No question. He hated it at night. He would look out of his window and see the trees either motionless or waving eerily against the horizon, illuminated by the light of the moon. It had a softly phosphorescent glow, but he didn't like it. It was spooky and he could imagine creatures creeping stealthily through the undergrowth and unspeakable things happening in the woods.

Sometimes he felt his mother *was* cracking up, and that if he wasn't careful he'd crack up too.

He lay in the dark aware of the silence, the pervasive, all-consuming silence, thinking. He wasn't a bit tired. He did so much lying about, watching TV or dozing during the day that he now slept quite badly at night. He often turned on the light again and read but tonight he didn't feel like it. He felt restless, and vengeful. He brooded on how much he hated Alan King.

Trouble was he'd always known his father was a little man, mentally that was; an emotionally timid man, easily bullied by people in a position over him. He supposed you couldn't have chosen the job he did unless you were. To Jake insurance seemed a con; safe, unimaginative, horribly dull. It was the sort of thing people did who couldn't do anything else. Ex-army officers with a plentiful supply of patter sold insurance, or men who had been unceremoniously turfed out of other jobs.

Jake had always known his mother was stronger, better

172

educated, with more personality, tied down by a man with whom she was mismatched. He loved his mother very much. He depended on her and between them was a strong bond. He sometimes felt he would like to free her from his pusillanimous and inadequate father, who could yet be a bit of a domestic bully, but she'd told Jake she would never leave his father because at her age she'd nowhere else to go and nothing to do. It was lack of opportunity rather than any belief in fidelity.

There was a scratch on the door. Jake cocked an ear. There it was again. He crept out of bed and over to the door without putting on the light, opened it a fraction, and Skittles slithered through, muttering away in cat language.

Jake picked her up and took her back to bed with him where, tail high, she walked up and down purring, kneading the duvet with pleasure.

"Where have you been?" he asked her finally snuggling his face against her body. "You keep on disappearing. I think you've got a boyfriend."

Skittles seemed to give him a coy, knowing look and climbing on to his chest, stared rather unnervingly into his eyes. She was, indeed, an extraordinarily handsome cat, a mysterious cat, the personification of the image of the cat who walked by itself: self-contained, aloof, alone.

"Skittles, you are responsible for a lot," he said taking her face between his hands and staring into her almond eyes. "If only you could talk. I wish you'd have been here earlier. You could have frightened that old bugger to death—"

Then he stopped, as a thought struck him.

Alan King tossed restlessly in the narrow bed in the spare room. The mattress was hard and the duvet kept slipping off the nylon sheets. He hated nylon sheets and he guessed these were a special offer from some discount store or the other.

Something about this whole house baffled him, worried him. It wasn't that it was just untidy, cheaply and tattily furnished – well that too – but there was something oppressive about the atmosphere. It was distinctly unhealthy, and his room smelt of something unpleasant, like drains. He raised himself on the bed and his nostrils twitched. Yes there it was again, an unhealthy whiff, as though the place had been built on a cesspool.

He glanced at his watch, saw that it was after one and tried to court sleep. No luck.

Then John worried him. He'd always slightly despised him as a nondescript person of no consequence, but he possessed undoubted ability in his job and brought in the business. Lots of business. He seemed to assume an altogether different personality when he was on the scent of a sale, and his record had fully justified his promotion. Yet John was a sycophant, easy to tread on, someone you could crush underfoot. However, he was making a success of the new branch, whatever his personal shortcomings. Business was good, above average for the time of year.

But why, and this was the puzzle, should he need money? To say he couldn't afford to move was absurd. Alan King's eyes narrowed in the dark. It was impossible to believe he was on some kind of fiddle, yet here, he felt, was something that needed investigation.

At last Alan King felt a weariness begin to overwhelm his overactive mind, and he was about to turn over and court the sleep he so craved when there was an ominous, unmistakable 'click'.

He sat up in bed, saw the door slowly opening. He smelt that god-awful, all-pervasive stench positively overwhelm him, and then a ghostly, furry body, seeming gigantic in size, jumped on his face and smothered him before he could even cry out.

Chapter Ten

"Is that you Helen?" Pauline asked.

"Yes it's me," Helen said. "Hi!"

"Hi! How's Mr King?"

"Oh he's much better."

"Thank God."

"Thank God. You can say that again."

"Awful if he'd have *died* on you."

Helen repressed a shudder. Apparently it wasn't a heart attack, just a seizure of some sort, but as he was so overweight and obviously unfit they kept him in hospital for observation.

"You must have been *ever* so worried."

"I'll say."

"John all right?"

"He wanted to have the cat put down."

"*No!*"

"Not the cat's fault if someone is afraid of it."

"But how did it get into the bedroom?"

Silence.

"Helen?"

"Yes?"

"How did it get into the bedroom?"

"No one quite knows. We think he must have left the door ajar."

"But if he's afraid of cats . . . doesn't make sense does it, with one in the house?"

"Look Pauline," Helen's tone had resumed its customary tension, the strain and anxiety that Pauline was used

175

to now every time she spoke to her. A strange, brittle tone; like someone on the verge of cracking up. "Why don't you come and stay for a few days? I could do with a friendly body."

Pauline's reaction was instinctive and immediate, as Helen had been rather afraid it might be.

"Not at the moment dear," she said. "Absolutely impossible to get away. Anyway, you know, Sharon still gets those headaches she started after we came back from you."

Silence again.

"Helen?"

"Yes I heard. The doctor thinks there may be something in the soil."

"The *soil*?"

"Environmental pollution, you know. You hear about it all the time."

"But why does she get them here?"

No answer.

"But look . . . when the school holidays begin why don't *you* come and stay with me? Bring Meg."

"But they squabbled so much."

"I'm sure they won't here. It's that place." Pauline paused, trying to think of a more tactful way to put it. "It's that atmosphere. Maybe there *is* something in the soil. You know what I mean."

"I know what you mean."

"Frankly, I think the sooner you get away the better."

"Not a chance."

"I mean for a few days."

"Oh! I'll think about it. Yes I really will."

"It will be lovely to see you again."

"And you."

Helen put down the phone with a sigh and, going over to the window, stood there for a long time gazing out into the garden, a subject on which she and John had had

176

their most recent row. He said that Alan King had been particularly critical about the garden and she had replied that if that was the case why didn't he, John, do something about it for God's sake? What with that coming on top of that awful visit, having to call an ambulance in the middle of the night . . . the after shocks of which were still reverberating.

Well she damn well didn't care about the tangled mess that was the garden *or* the tip that was, at the moment, the house or . . . suddenly she wondered what would happen if she simply packed her things and left home. Packed up, went away, vanished, disappeared. Not say anything to anyone, not even the children. Leave them all to it. Other women had done it. Maybe she'd take Skittles to save her from the certain death that was bound to follow if she left her to John's tender mercies.

But the poor cat. Really. It wasn't her fault. It was *Jake's* fault and he had done it quite deliberately, Helen was sure of that. It was the way he just smiled and waggled his head when she'd asked him directly, "Well, did you open the door or didn't you?"

She'd probably never know. He'd never dare say.

She, Helen, knew perfectly well that Alan would never have gone to bed and left the door open. For one thing you didn't do that in another person's house. The door would have been tightly shut, and as she knew neither she nor John had opened it and Meg was away it could only have been Jake, who didn't like Alan King. Well neither did she. None of them did. She suspected that John actually hated him, but was too two-faced to say so. Two-faced and frightened and, now, frankly terrified because of what had happened to his boss on the night of the visit.

Yes it was very tempting just to up and go. To throw off all her responsibilities. And what would she do for money? Maybe she could get her old job back and work full time.

This brought her back to reality, and Pauline. Far more sensible, after all, to retreat to Worcester Park with Meg and the cat. The other had been a rash, ridiculous flight of fantasy . . . way, way out.

The sight of a car rounding the corner by Muriel's and then crawling along, as though looking for a house, interrupted her reverie. She watched it apathetically at first, then with increasing interest and curiosity as it stopped outside her gate.

There were two men in the car and they seemed to consult something between them for quite some time before looking at the house, at her standing in the window – she didn't try to hide, why should she? Then each one got out on his own side before they joined up together by her gate, pushed it open and came up the path.

Helen watched them with mounting alarm, and when they rang the doorbell she remained where she was. Tempests' luck. She knew, was convinced, that this was yet another portent of disaster; the latest in a never-ending series of dark, sinister happenings to visit the house.

The bell rang again and, knowing they must have seen her, that it was useless to pretend not to be in, she made a robust effort to pull herself together – a task she did several times, almost daily – and made her way to the front door. But she didn't open it. Who were these men after all? She was alone in the house.

"Who is it?" she called softly.

There was silence which seemed to justify her apprehension. Then: "It's the police madam. Please don't be alarmed. Routine enquiry."

"How do I know you're the police?"

"We have identification, madam, if you'd open the door."

"Or we can show you through the window," a second voice broke in, "where you were standing just now."

Helen opened the door and saw that the men, looking

178

slightly apologetic, had their identity cards displayed in the palms of their hands. Helen only gave them a cursory glance.

"What sort of routine enquiry?" She didn't ask them in.

"May we come in Mrs . . ." one of the policemen consulted a paper in his hand, "is it Mrs Tempest?"

"I am Mrs Tempest." A hand clasped her breast. "Please tell me what's wrong? Is it my husband?"

"It is nothing to do with you madam," the first police officer said in a reassuring tone. "*Nothing* about which you should alarm yourself in any way. No harm done to any member of your family. This concerns something else entirely."

Helen stepped back and beckoned them into the living room.

"Excuse the mess," she said, vaguely indicating the room in general but specifically the kitchen where the breakfast things still stood where they'd been left on the breakfast bar. "I haven't been well."

She had her housecoat wrapped tightly around her. Pale and pinched-looking, she certainly gave the impression of a sick woman. The men grimaced sympathetically.

"Detective Inspector Jarvis," the man who had spoken first pointed to himself before turning to his companion. "Detective Constable Morgan."

Helen nodded for them to sit down.

Inspector Jarvis produced a notebook from his pocket and flipped over the pages.

"It's about the people who were here before you, Mrs Tempest."

"The Beckets," Helen cried with a catch in her voice.

"That's right." The policeman looked up sharply. "Did you know them?"

"No I didn't but, of course, we knew the circumstances in which they left . . ."

179

"And that was . . . ?" Constable Morgan looked interested.

"Well . . ." she faltered, "the house was repossessed."

His face registered disappointment. "And that was all you knew?"

"Of course. We never met them. I . . ." she gazed down at her hands which she continually clenched and unclenched, "I didn't particularly *like* buying a house that had been forcibly taken away from someone else."

"Many people feel like that madam," the Inspector said politely.

"Oh do they? Good. I mean . . . my husband thought I was silly."

"Not at all, merely compassionate."

"Oh well, thanks." Helen pushed her hair back from her hot, sticky brow. "I'm glad to hear it."

"But the reason we are here, Mrs Tempest, is that no one appears to have seen Mrs Susan Becket since she left, and we are making routine enquiries as to her whereabouts."

"No one has *seen* her?" Helen felt her pulse quicken.

"Her husband says she left home after a family row and he thinks she is living abroad. But her parents and sister think she would have been in touch with them, would not have wished necessarily to have upset them or her children, so we've begun an enquiry."

Helen thought guiltily back to her wandering thoughts a few moments before; her wish for flight, to disappear leaving husband *and* children behind. Maybe Susan Becket had acted out her fantasies. If so, how well she understood her.

Helen put her hand to her mouth. "But I don't see how I can help?"

"Just to enquire if she came back here for any reason?" Constable Morgan looked round the room. "Did she, for instance, telephone you?"

180

"No. Not at all. I've never had anything to do with them."

"Or him? Mr Becket never came back?"

"Not that I know of. Not to this house. Also . . ." she hesitated, pulling her lip, "they appeared not to know many people here, if any. But my neighbour Muriel Forbes did know them slightly."

"Oh? That's interesting." Inspector Jarvis looked over his shoulder. "Would she be in do you know?"

"I don't think she is." Helen gazed across the road. "The garage doors are open and her car's not there. But I'm pretty sure she's had no contact with them since they left. She would have told me."

"And the neighbours? Any other neighbours?" The two detectives exchanged glances.

"They keep themselves pretty much to themselves. We really only know Miss Forbes. Most of the others work. They're out all day, busy at weekends. I'm pretty sure none of them knew the Beckets; but the best time would be to call round at weekends or in the evenings. You're sure to find someone in then."

"Thank you very much Mrs Tempest." Inspector Jarvis rose, followed by his subordinate. "I'm very sorry to have bothered you and, perhaps, frightened you."

"Oh you didn't frighten me." Helen too rose. "Only such a lot has happened here recently, none of it nice. My son had an accident and then a couple of weeks ago a friend staying in the house nearly had a heart attack. I thought you might be from the hospital to say he was dead or something. You know one feels apprehensive all the time." And she drew her housecoat even more tightly, protectively, around her.

She thought the detectives must have considered her an object of pity. She didn't blame them. She probably was.

"I'm so sorry, madam, but we must have given you a bit of a turn." Inspector Jarvis looked concerned as she

181

showed them to the front door. There he stood gazing round the garden with those same alert, probing eyes as if noting the fact that, like the interior of the house, the outside was also in need of care and attention. The grass was about a foot high, the flower beds thick with weeds, the roses riddled with rust and blackspot, and greenfly and blackfly everywhere. A sorry sight. He opened his notebook once again. "Exactly when did you move in Mrs Tempest?"

"About ten months ago. We moved in last September."

"September," the Inspector noted carefully in his notebook, "and now it's July. Nearly a year."

"Nearly a year," she agreed.

Nearly a year into which to make this place into a home, she bet he thought . . . and so far she hadn't.

Mr Carr leafed through the file in front of him.

"So you decided to move after all Miss Forbes? Sooner than you expected, perhaps?"

Muriel nodded nervously several times. Really she was so edgy herself these days. Whatever it was that was happening to the Tempests appeared to be catching. Environmental pollution seemed such a far-fetched idea. But it did make one wonder sometimes if there was any truth in these notions. Maybe the whole of the hill, an ancient burial ground after all, was full of age-old germs?

"I'm not *unhappy*," she realized she must have sounded unconvincing, "it's just not what I want. Not really. Too far from friends. I've hardly any family, and friends are important you know."

"Oh they are."

"I'm always away."

"Property's very slow at the moment." Mr Carr clicked his tongue. "You might have it on your hands for some time. Where were you thinking of going?"

182

"I think nearer the sea. Maybe Poole or Bournemouth."

"Very nice," Mr Carr nodded approvingly. "Oh, by the way, we had a visit from the police."

Muriel reacted sharply. "About the Beckets? So did I. I told them it wouldn't surprise *me* if she had left home. They were always having terrible rows. The policeman seemed quite interested."

"I know absolutely nothing about them."

"But you sold them the house."

"We seem, in fact, to have handled most of the sales in the years since it was built," he scratched his chin pensively, "as I think I told you. Quite a lot of people have moved in and out in thirty years. After the police had gone I was looking—"

"Oh do you think *I* might have a look?" Muriel interjected eagerly. "You know sometimes I've wondered if there was *something* in what Helen Tempest said: that a place could actually be infected by the people who lived there . . ."

As Mr Carr looked at her strangely, confidence in her theory evaporated. "You know," she continued lamely, "and made unhappy."

"It's a very ordinary sort of house Miss Forbes." Carr's tone was now disapproving.

"I know. That's what I told Helen."

"Well the Beckets certainly weren't very happy people. He did his best to stop having it repossessed. He was an architect and felt it reflected on him professionally . . . which it would. In fact, I think it did and they moved right away."

"And who was before the Beckets?" Muriel decided to press home her advantage.

Carr continued to leaf through his file, pausing every now and then to study a document as though reluctant to pursue the scent.

"A Mr and Mrs Knowles." He looked up. "I think you might have known them."

Muriel shook her head. "I believe they were quite old."

"That's why he moved. The wife died. The next people—"

"Did she die there?" Muriel asked a little apprehensively.

"In the house? I wouldn't know . . ."

"I mean, if she did—"

"You're thinking of ghosts again?" The corners of Mr Carr's mouth twitched.

"Not at all."

"I think she died in a nursing home."

"No idea which one?"

"Really Miss Forbes," Carr wagged a finger at her, his good humour clearly returning, "I'm afraid you're beginning to let your imagination run away with you. Now . . ." he continued his inspection of the file, "we didn't handle the sale before that, or the one before *that*. I think your best bet, if you're really curious and, frankly, it seems to me rather a waste of time, *is* the Land Registry."

"Oh I wouldn't dream of it," Muriel waved a dismissive hand, "it was just a vague notion I had."

Carr drew a fresh piece of paper towards him. "Now, if I might take the particulars of your house, and then, maybe, fix an appointment with you to come up and measure, though I think I probably already have the details."

"Please don't let Helen Tempest see you when you do," Muriel lowered her voice urgently. "I'd hate her to know that I'm even thinking of leaving. I think she really might crack up then."

Muriel was brooding on the notion of cracking up in the car on the way home. Who wouldn't crack up with neighbours like the Tempests and, before them, people like the Beckets, about whom even the police were now curious? Sometimes the cries and screams that came floating over the road from the house opposite, when the Beckets were in residence, made her feel that murder was in the air. She'd told the police so too.

Frankly she wouldn't have been surprised if Ralph Becket *had* done his wife in, and the sooner *she*, Muriel got away from this district the better. The place was getting on her nerves.

She'd liked Helen well enough, but she couldn't really call her life her own. She found herself creeping in and out, hoping she wouldn't be seen, in case Helen wanted anything; sometimes just to chat, usually merely needing comfort.

Mr Carr had suggested that she consult the Land Registry if she wanted to know who were the occupants of number fourteen since it was built. But if she did, so what? Even if she discovered the names of half a dozen couples, or individuals, it would be almost impossible to know what sort of lives they had led, what had happened to them. They would be names on a computer screen, nothing more. There was the woman who died, but death came at the end to everyone. Grumpily Muriel decided she was wasting her time and, instead of thinking continually about the wretched Tempests, she should be thinking about herself.

It was thus in rather a bad temper that Muriel reached her home and sat in her car outside her house staring across at the Tempest garden, grass a foot high, weeds all over the place.

She thought she definitely must steel herself to ask Helen to do something about the garden, at least get her husband to cut the lawn and generally tidy up.

Muriel's eyes wandered across her own, well-tended green lawn, the colourful herbaceous borders, an ornamental pond dotted with goldfish and presided over by a family of garden gnomes. The Tempest garden had become a talking point among the neighbours, who scarcely ever spoke to one another about anything at all.

185

Muriel wondered if she should bite the bullet and go and discuss the matter with Helen now and get it over; but she decided she was in too uneven a mood to undertake such a task. She might lose control of her well-known serenity, her evenness of temper considering all the toing and froing she was doing on behalf of the wretched family at the moment. It had, she decided, become a kind of obsession and she must stop. She would go indoors and make herself a cup of tea and then decide what to do.

Muriel left the car outside the house – she was going out in the evening – and, unloading her parcels, went inside. On the mat by the front door there was a folded sheet of paper with her name on it. She went through the hall and put the groceries on the kitchen table, before returning to the hall and picking up the note which she scanned as she went into the living room to find her reading spectacles. She finally found them and sat down abruptly, unable momentarily to take in what the note said:

'Dear Muriel,
This is to tell you that I have left John temporarily while I try and sort myself out. We have been going through a very bad time – worse than usual – and the business with Alan King didn't help at all. I feel completely worn out, as you're probably aware. Jake is at the scout camp for another few weeks, and I have taken Meg with me. We are going to Pauline's and I'll telephone you in a day or two.
Love, Helen.

PS. I was unable to find Skittles who has done another bunk. If you find her, do you think you could look after her, because John *wants to have her destroyed*?'

Muriel read the note through twice more and then put

186

it on the table, her own emotions in turmoil. She felt Helen might have confided her intentions to her, and then – of all the cheek – expecting her to look after the *cat* without even having the courtesy of first telling her she was *going*!

Now that wretched garden would *have* to be done. Well perhaps if things had come to this they would soon be selling the house anyway.

Muriel certainly hoped so. Then she might take hers off the market and make a superhuman effort to try to settle down again, resume her pleasant, routine-filled life, as it was before the Tempests arrived.

John stood patiently in the queue by the betting shop window and, when his turn came, slipped two fifty pound notes under the grille.

"Fair Penelope at 10–1," he said. "To win."

The clerk looked at him, took the two notes, examined them and gave him his slip without comment. The look seemed to tell him he considered he was throwing his money away.

Well he would see. This was the big day. This was the day on which he was going to try his luck on the final Treble. He had never been able to pull it off before, and lately the horses hadn't been going his way. But he had studied the form book, calculated the odds. It was a small stake and if Fair Penelope failed to win he'd chuck the whole thing in. He might even do a runner himself and disappear.

He stood in a corner of the betting shop, apparently calm but smoking a lot, shoulders hunched, studying the form for the next race.

As the starter gave the orders he ground his cigarette under his heel and put his hands deep in his pockets, realizing how clammy they were. His only sign of nerves. Fair Penelope wasn't mentioned for the first few furlongs, until near the end of the race the commentator's voice began to scream with excitement . . . Fair Penelope coming up on the side. Fair Penelope had done it.

"You were lucky," the clerk murmured, counting out eleven hundred pounds. "Had a tip-off did you?"

John didn't reply, his mind concentrating on the job in hand. He had to back three winners at the same meeting and the odds were heavily against him.

"I want to put it all on Lucky Streak at 8–1 to win." He pushed the money back towards the bookie.

"Lucky streak at 8–1," the bookie said, reclaimed the money and gave John his slip.

This time the waiting was less easy. Lucky Streak had to have a lucky streak for him, or his life lay in ruins. Unless he repaid the money he had stolen everything would be discovered when the books were audited, and now that Alan King was on the mend he might remember their conversation the night before he was taken ill. Lucky Streak was John's only chance.

This time he turned his back to the room so that he avoided seeing the apprehensive faces of the other punters, or the TV set in the corner on which the race was being televised.

Lucky Streak fulfilled his promise. The betting clerk counted out eight thousand pounds, less tax, and told John he was a very lucky man.

John ignored the tribute. "I want it all on My Alison to win." Showing no emotion he slid the money under the grille.

"The odds are 7–2," the bookie said – as if he didn't know. John nodded. This time he had an uncanny instinct that he had it in the bag, but he still felt a sense of wild elation as the horse came cantering in, an easy winner as it turned out, bringing John a total win of thirty thousand eight hundred pounds,less ten per cent betting tax.

Now they could move. He could go straight, repay

the money, reset the accounts, close down the phoney company, and hide all evidence of his misdemeanour. They could get out of that accursed house and go the other side of Yeovil where Helen had seen a house she liked.

John Tempest was a complex man, categorized by his peers as 'boring' ever since he could remember, dull and diffident – he knew what they said – and he had always nursed a grudge, waited for the opportunity to strike out and show his detractors a thing or two.

His first unexpected success was persuading Helen to marry him. At the time he thought it was a coup. Only when he got to know her did he realize how insecure she was with a domineering mother she was glad to get away from.

John had always been neat, meticulous, liking things in their places, hating surprises. Insurance was the sort of safe, solid job he liked. He enjoyed figures and was good at them.

It was his head for figures that first introduced him to racing. He had a friend called Bob Hewitt who was far more dashing and daring than he was, impulsive and a risk taker. Despite their dissimilarities he'd rather envied Bob, his flair, his prowess with girls. Bob was also a great gambler and John began to enjoy challenging Bob by studying form and showing statistically how one horse was more capable of winning than another, without having a flutter himself.

Bob Hewitt eventually quietened down, married and went to live in the north of England. John lost touch with him but he continued to find the study of form fascinating, especially as it was a secret from everyone else, including his wife. Surreptitiously, at first, he risked a bet at short odds, and then another, gradually lengthening them and increasing the odds. It was heady stuff.

John was an addictive personality but few people seemed to realize it. He smoked too much and his war games and collection of war posters were a mild form of addiction. There was little to indicate to anyone a reckless passion for racing, though it should have been obvious because of his self-proclaimed shortage of money. But no one believed him and called him a miser.

Like many people with a secret vice, John enjoyed the secrecy, cherished it, and also the fact that no one knew, not even his wife. It was like being a secret drinker, being another John.

Steadily over the years his income declined as, inevitably, he lost more than he won. His system could never be foolproof. But he couldn't stop and by the time they moved to Dorset it had reached dangerous proportions. The move was a failure, family life became a misery, but John simply gambled more than ever and finally he started to steal.

Helen's health began to persuade him he had overdone it, gone too far. In his odd way he loved his wife, needed her and the little stability she and the family gave him. It was time to call a halt, make a new beginning. It was never too late to draw back. He had often dreamed of winning the Treble, the jackpot, but he'd only ended up losing, sometimes thousands. Today for a mere one hundred pounds stake he had won just over thirty thousand pounds. He had brought it off, and he couldn't tell a soul.

As he slowed down to take the road to Tip Hollow the idle thought struck him that it *did* make you wonder if you might just go on for a bit more and, having done it once, see if he could really make it to the big time.

He'd stopped off in Sherborne to buy Helen a huge bunch of flowers. It was many years since he'd been so generous. He might also suggest that tonight or, perhaps tomorrow, they should go out for dinner. Hard to remember when they'd last done that too. He thought bought flowers unnecessarily expensive and dining out, when you could eat at home for a fraction of the cost, downright extravagant. It was this that had got him his reputation for parsimoniousness.

But now they would definitely be able to make a new beginning. And for him, who had so nearly been over the edge, it would be a relief to put his past behind him. He didn't say he would *never* gamble again, but it would only be a flutter every now and then. A pound each way, or maybe five . . . A few pounds on the Lottery.

He grinned to himself. It was really very difficult to think in such small terms when you had pulled off the Treble and had close on thirty thousand pounds in your pocket.

John reaching home, parked the car outside the house, noticing that Muriel hadn't garaged hers either. He didn't like her very much. He thought she was self-centred, censorious, and a bad and disturbing influence on Helen. Well with any luck they would soon be leaving her behind too; nosy old Muriel, and all the unfriendly, bumptious neighbours on the exclusive Tip Hollow estate.

John got out of the car and, the large bunch of flowers clasped to his chest, went up the garden path towards the house.

The grass was very long. Alan King would have a fit if he saw it which, hopefully, he never would. He had come out of hospital and was convalescing at a home in Brighton at the expense of the company. By the time he was fit and well John would have the books at the Yeovil office in apple-pie order and there might even be a little left aside for himself.

He pushed the door but it was locked. He rang the doorbell, but no one came. With a sigh of irritation he produced his keys from his pocket and, selecting the Yale key for the front door, put it in the lock and turned.

"Hello!" he called out cheerily. "I'm home."

No reply.

"Helen . . . Meg?"

No sound; only miaowing. That damn cat . . . if he caught it, but no . . . it would irreparably harm his relationship with Helen and above all Meg, whose cat it really was. Besides he felt now in too good a humour, much too good to wish harm to the family pet.

He went into the sitting room, putting the flowers carefully down on the table. A brief glance in the kitchen not only confirmed that neither Helen nor Meg were there, but that the breakfast things hadn't been touched. Frankly the kitchen was in a tip. Dirty.

His good humour began to evaporate as he inspected the chaos and he went back into the hall, taking off his jacket and throwing it over the banister as he went upstairs to the bedroom he shared with Helen. This too was in disorder, the bed unmade, cupboards open.

He suddenly began to feel uneasy, thinking about those awful things one read about a man going home to find his wife and family murdered. Much as one enjoyed reading about them, incidents like that had always seemed far fetched and impossible to visualize. Not, perhaps, so much now.

He began to feel a flicker of fear and moved rapidly through the house: the bedroom – Meg's bedroom too in disorder and her bed unmade – the bathroom, the spare room, and, finally, down to the sitting room where, rather wildly, he looked around.

Then he spotted an envelope on the small table by the side of the window, propped up against the leather cigarette box they'd bought in Italy on their honeymoon. He took up the letter, saw his name written on it, sat down and opened it.

'Dear John,

I have gone off with Meg for a while to stay with Pauline. I don't know when I'll be back or if I will. I've felt so ill for the last few weeks, so hated Tip Hollow and the house, that I don't think I can take

192

any more. I decided this morning on an impulse to go. I rang Pauline, but didn't tell Muriel though I've left her a note and asked her to look after Skittles. If you harm her, John, that's just another of the things I'll have against you.

Obviously we must meet and talk, but please give me a few days to think things through. There's plenty in the freezer for you to eat.'

It was just signed 'Helen'. No 'love', no 'yours'. Just Helen. She might as well have signed it Mrs Tempest.

John sat back and closed his eyes. He felt utterly lost and rejected. From upstairs came the sound of miaowing and he thought perhaps the wretched cat had got itself caught somewhere. Good. Perhaps it would starve.

There was a tap at the door and a shadow fell over the hallway.

"May I come in?" Muriel called, peering round the door, her face almost as crestfallen as John's.

"She's not here," John said.

"I know." Muriel diffidently ventured further into the room. "I got a note. I'm . . . *terribly* sorry, John." She perched on the very edge of the seat opposite him, wringing her hands in an ingratiating, irritating way.

"Sorry about what?" he asked coldly. "She's just gone to visit her friend."

He stared at her as if daring her to contradict him. There came the sound of miaowing again, more urgently this time, and Muriel looked enquiringly towards the stairs.

"She said she couldn't *find* Skittles."

"Well she's upstairs somewhere."

"Should I go and look?"

"There's no need to be worried about Skittles, you know. She's the house cat and I am *perfectly* capable of looking after her."

"Oh of *course*!" Muriel stood up. "Just wanted to be

helpful. Let me know if you need anything John, and John . . . I hate to mention it now, because I can see how tired you are, but *do* you think you could get round to cutting the grass? It looks so untidy. People are beginning to complain I'm afraid . . ."

John didn't throw her out but he felt like it and, taking her cue, Muriel fled.

John tried to get through to Pauline but she had taken the phone off the hook. He tidied the kitchen, put the dirty dishes in the dishwasher and made himself beans on toast. He went upstairs to look for the cat but couldn't find her. He opened all the doors, cupboards, looked under the bed. There was no crevice or aperture she could possibly have slipped into or through. A window was open, however, in Meg's room so he shut it. He pulled her duvet over the bed and did the same with his. Looking across the road he caught sight of Muriel staring at him. When she saw him looking she quickly stepped back from the window.

She was watching the bloody house. She was a typical nosy parker busybody who had nothing better to do with her time. Muriel alone would be a very good reason for getting out of Tip Hollow.

At ten John watched the news, without seeing it, and when it had finished he prepared to retire.

He had a last look round for Skittles, but she was nowhere to be found. He left her food and milk outside the kitchen door, locked up and went to bed.

All through the night he tossed restlessly, waking often and imagining he could hear the pathetic miaowing of a cat trapped helplessly inside the walls.

Chapter Eleven

Helen lay in bed, head resting on her arms, the sun shining through the window, the cat asleep on the bottom of the bed. Perfect. No worries. No headaches, no awful shuddery fits or panic attacks. No sleeplessness, waking in the middle of the night with those ghastly, black depressions.

Above all, no John.

Maybe John was at the root of her problems, and it wasn't the house at all? Pauline's latest theory was that this was the solution. The immediate change in Helen had been so marked. Maybe she'd taken the problem of their marriage with her and, somehow, all this had focused onto the house. The only really worrying, really spooky thing was that episode with Mrs Markham. Whatever Pauline's views, freely given, Helen was sure her experience was real, and when she thought about it she could find no explanation that was not deeply, profoundly disturbing.

If only Skittles could speak. She nudged the cat with her toe. Skittles half opened her eyes, raised her head and then tucked it more comfortably between her paws. Bliss.

Skittles, mysterious cat. What could she not tell her about that strange episode? How *glad* she was that she'd brought Skittles with her. Just before they left, the taxi standing waiting for them at the gate, Skittles had sauntered nonchalantly round the corner with the air of one out to enjoy the sun. With a cry of relief

Helen had scooped the cat up, tucked her in her basket and carried her away. No time to change her notes.

John didn't matter but she really *must* ring Muriel and tell her she had the cat. But she was very reluctant to break into her exile and ring anyone from that part of the world, anyone who had a link with her unhappy past. John eventually got through but she wouldn't speak to him. Pauline was more than capable of dealing with John who, Helen knew, was rather scared of her formidable, faithful friend.

She could hear stirring in the passage outside; the door opened and Meg slid into the room.

"You awake Mummy?"

"Wide awake." Helen smiled at her and put out her hand. "Did you sleep well?"

"Very well. Did Skittles sleep well?" Meg went over to the cat and, stretching herself beside her, began to stroke her. Skittles stretched her paws stiffly in front of her, a half smile on her face. "Do you think she likes it here, Mummy?"

"She's settled very well."

"Aren't you frightened she'll run away?"

"We won't let her out too soon. It's very kind of Pauline to have us and the cat."

"I'd like to stay here, Mummy, wouldn't you?"

"Here, with Pauline?"

"Well not necessarily, but here in Worcester Park."

Worcester Park, sandwiched between arterial roads servicing the capital in the heart of suburbia, was not perhaps the most beautiful place in the world but, yes, it was home. It was the place they knew, where they had their friends, where Meg had been born.

"What about Daddy?" Helen asked, a catch in her voice.

Meg was silent, continuing to press her head into Skittles' furry coat until the cat began to tire of the attention and her tail started whisking angrily up and down.

196

"You're suffocating her." Helen reached out to push Meg away from the animal, who vigorously licked the spot on her coat where Meg had pressed her head. Strange animals, cats. It was as though sometimes they resented the love and attention that at other times they craved.

"Daddy and I might split for good," Helen announced suddenly. Meg nodded as if she understood. "Would you mind?"

Meg shook her head.

"The rows got on my nerves, Jake's too. What will happen to Jake, Mummy? Will he stay with Daddy?"

"Oh no," the idea appalled her, "and I'm not *sure* that Daddy and I will split up for good. I just wanted to know how you felt. After all, we've been married a long time, and then there's the money. I'd have to earn my own living. Oh there are all sorts of things to consider. Meanwhile this is a breathing space."

"Anyone for the bathroom before I go in?" Pauline put her head round the door.

Helen waved at her. Oh it was so *nice* to be with Pauline again.

Helen was like a new woman, Pauline thought, as she came into the room surveying the cosy domestic scene although they'd only been here a few days. That terrible stretched appearance of her skin, like old leather, the habitual expression of anxiety had almost gone. She was putting on weight again, drinking less. At night after she'd first arrived they'd both rather hit the bottle.

"I'm going to have a pee," Meg announced.

"You run along then and ask Sharon if she wants to use the bathroom before me." Pauline settled on the side of Helen's bed with a smile. No rows between the girls now. All sweetness and harmony, she seemed to say.

"Sleep well?"

"Fabulous!" Helen stretched again, her fingers touching the head of the bed. "It's ever so *good* of you to have us here Pauline."

"You know I like it. I like the company. Sharon loves having Meg. You can stay as long as you like, honestly, even when Jake comes back from scout camp. But," she paused, "at some stage something has got to be sorted out with John. Some decision has to be made about Fourteen Tip Hollow Hill. You know you can't live in a state of suspended animation for ever."

John's eyes were bloodshot. He scarcely slept at nights and now he had started developing the headaches. He hated living on his own and he hated the house. It was a creepy house where everything creaked at night and, though he no longer heard noises, he was haunted by the idea that somehow the cat had been trapped somewhere inside and was dead. He now blamed the house for a great deal; for the fact that Helen had nearly had a nervous breakdown, and for the break-up of his marriage. It was quite true: a house had a soul.

He peered at himself in the shaving mirror, turning down the corner of each bloodshot eye with his fore-finger. He looked terrible. He felt terrible. He wanted Helen and Meg back; he wanted the family life which he now knew he had not appreciated at the time.

He finished shaving, did his teeth, rinsed his mouth out with gargle and swallowed two Paracetamol tablets with water.

He went back to the bedroom, saw the time and dressed rapidly. He used always to make a point of being in before the staff, but now he was invariably the last. He knew that somehow morale in the office had changed, and it was not a happy place. The staff resented him, looked at him warily, avoided him if they could. He was so tetchy, difficult to deal with and he suspected most of them guessed Helen had left him, though he had told everyone she was on holiday. Somehow truth had a way of getting out.

John ran swiftly down the stairs to the kitchen, popped

two slices of bread into the toaster and flicked on the kettle. He ran his hands over his head. The place was in a terrible mess. He would simply have to get someone in to give it a thorough clean. He was so whacked at night when he got home that he just slumped in front of the TV, had a TV dinner and went to bed. He invariably fell asleep in front of the TV, but once he was in bed he was wide awake and it continued on and off like that all night.

A shadow appeared by the back door and he flung it open. Muriel! Of course.

"I'm awfully *sorry*, John . . ."

"What is it Muriel?" he asked.

"Any news from Helen?"

"No."

"Oh!" Muriel's hand fluttered nervously to her hair.

"I *do* think it's funny she hasn't contacted *me*."

"Why should she contact you Muriel?" His patience was on the verge of exhaustion too.

"Because she asked *me* to look after the cat."

"Well the cat isn't here. It's lost. And good riddance."

"Oh!" She looked at him suspiciously. "You *haven't* . . . ?"

"Haven't *what* Muriel?" The toast popped out of the toaster and he rushed back into the kitchen. "Haven't what? Look I'm late for work."

"Well you haven't . . ."

"Haven't done away with the cat? No, I haven't and I haven't *done away with my wife either* if that's what you're thinking."

John then slammed the kitchen door in her face enjoying her expression of outrage as she saw it close.

From the corner of the sitting room, well away from the window, Muriel watched him back the car out into the road and drive away with a screech of tyres. She was filled with deep foreboding. She thought it extremely odd

199

she hadn't heard from Helen, there was *no* sign of the cat, and the police were nosing round again. Yesterday they had spent a lot of time looking over the fence at the garden of number fourteen. That's the real reason she had gone to see John that morning but he had been so *rude*, really offensive. So, let him find out for himself.

She thought it was really quite extraordinarily bizarre that the Tempest saga seemed to imitate so much what she knew about the life of the Beckets . . . and now both wives had gone missing! Perhaps she ought to tell the police about Helen?

Well that night she would ask John for Pauline's number, even if he did slam the door in her face again.

Muriel was restless, unhappy. The fate of the Tempests obsessed her, as did that of the cat. She had wandered round the village looking for Skittles, even penetrated quite deeply in the wood – heart pounding – in her attempt to find her. She was more convinced than ever that John had had her destroyed. He had never forgiven her for nearly frightening his boss quite literally to death and scuppering his chances of promotion.

It was the end of August, autumnal. Nearly a year since the Tempests had moved in. She remembered the van coming followed by the car; the children running up the garden. Skittles in her basket. It had seemed so *good* to have nice neighbours. What a letdown! And what a tremendous amount seemed to have happened in that time. Not only had their lives been affected, but hers had too, for the worse. She was no longer that happy, carefree, cheerful, well-behaved retired schoolmistress she once had been. She was now a nervous wreck, teetering, she felt, on the brink of old age with more grey hairs than she would have believed possible appearing in a year.

She looked out at her well-tended garden, around at her beautifully kept house, and compared both with the state of the Tempests! The kitchen, as she'd glimpsed it that morning, looked as though it hadn't been touched since

Helen had left. The grass was *well* over a foot high and there were masses of wild foxgloves dwarfing what few flowers were left. Wild foxgloves were very pretty, but they had no place in a domestic garden, not in her opinion anyway, though some people thought otherwise.

She wandered restlessly out into the garden with a pair of secateurs, snipping off the occasional dead head from her rose bushes. It was a greyish kind of day, definitely with more than a hint of autumn. In a month it would almost be winter.

She raised her head and looked over at the house of her neighbours. She thought, but couldn't be sure, that her eyes had detected movement in the knee-high grass. A little trickle of fear ran down her back for which she reprimanded herself. Probably a rabbit feasting, with some justification, on the lush fodder. And then with a profound sense of shock she knew: Skittles was back.

So as not to frighten her – and frighten herself since that encounter in the wood on the day of Jake's accident – she stood silently watching as the grey shape made its way through the tall grass to emerge at the end of the path by the gate.

The cat looked extremely well, not bedraggled or unkempt as one might expect had it been trapped somewhere, or lived rough. If anything she looked a bit fatter than before. She squatted down in the middle of the path, looked around her with evident satisfaction at being back, and commenced an elaborate toilet, as if she had all the time in the world. After a while she paused and gazed straight ahead of her, as if seeing Muriel for the first time.

Muriel went rather timidly to the fence, extended her hand in a placatory gesture, flicking her fingers, and calling in a wheeling tone, "Hello Skittles. Here kitty, kitty, kitty."

Skittles seemed to find the diversion amusing and, with sinuous grace, climbed on to the garden gate, balanced for a second and, jumping over the other side, strolled languidly towards Muriel as if she was actually quite pleased to see her.

Muriel hesitated, then opened the gate to let the cat in, and as she strolled through she bent tentatively to stroke her head.

"Skittles . . . where've you been, you naughty girl? You had us all worried."

Skittles sat and looked at her with an expression of amused contempt on her face, her secret safe.

It was mid-afternoon and the day hadn't got any better. There were problems with accounts, two members of staff off sick and the announcement that Alan King, now home after his convalescence, was intending to pay him another visit. This time there was no question of where to stay. He asked to be booked into a local hotel.

John felt that at this precarious stage of his life he simply couldn't bear a visit from Alan King, and he began looking up the holiday rota to see if he could wangle a few days' leave and let his deputy deal with the hated boss.

Like the rest of his family, John had never liked King, always resented him and his bullying ways. Yet for some reason he knew that he found favour with the ogre. Well, had until recently. King had always encouraged him, patronized him, given him a leg up. As they were opposed in temperament, had nothing in common, John had never known why King favoured him; except that he had an exceptional nose for the insurance market.

Or, he had been before his transfer to Yeovil.

There was a tap at his door and his deputy, Stewart Long, put his head round.

"Oh Stewart," John said, looking up, "I was just studying the holiday rota. I wondered if—"

"John," Stewart seemed ill at ease, "there are two blokes here to see you. I think they're from the police."

"The police?" John involuntarily clutched the front of his desk, betraying his agitation.

"I hope there's nothing wrong John." Stewart's voice was anxious. "Helen all right? Everything all right at home?"

"You'd better show them in." John regained his non-chalance. "Hope they won't take up too much of my time."

The policemen were ushered in by Stewart and there were polite nods all round.

"How do you do?"

"How do you do?"

"Detective Inspector Jarvis, Detective Constable Morgan."

"Nice to meet you."

Handshakes, coats removed. The men sat down. John, facing them, at his desk, wondered if they could see the rapid pulse in his neck. He put one hand over it, the sweaty palm of the other on the blotter in front of him.

"How can I help you gentlemen?"

"Well," Inspector Jarvis ran his finger round his collar, "I'm afraid we're here on rather a serious matter," and John knew that he knew. The prison gate began swinging shut.

"I paid the money back you know."

"I *beg* your pardon sir?" Subtle change of expression from Jarvis.

"I paid back every penny. You can see in the books for yourself. It may *look* a trifle irregular but it is all there."

Jarvis looked for a moment at his junior. "We are here, Mr Tempest, about the disappearance of Mrs Becket."

"Mrs who?" The prick of fear sharpened.

"Mr and Mrs Becket lived in the house you now occupy before you sir."

"Well *I* had nothing to do with the disappearance of Mrs Becket."

"We didn't think you had sir. As your wife seems to

be away, we merely came to ask your permission to make a thorough examination of your house and, if necessary, excavate the garden."

The police arrived two days later. First came a car with the two men whom she'd seen before, then came some trucks and more men who began slowly to measure out the garden.

For two nights John had not come home because Muriel had been dying to tell him about Skittles, who now appeared to have settled in; so she desperately wanted to telephone Helen to tell her all was well with the cat.

However John must have come home some time during the night because when she got up his car was there. She hurriedly had her bath and was dressing when the first official car arrived and John opened the door to let the men in.

She sat by the window with Skittles watching every move, everything that happened the entire morning. She was of course dying to rush over and find out what was going on, yet knowing John's temper she didn't dare. A number of men went into the house at about eleven, and then John came out and stood talking in the garden to one of the men, pointing over at the shed and moving his finger around.

It was all most mysterious, but at the same time extremely exciting.

John was about to go back to the house when he appeared to change his mind, came back into the garden and walked right up to his gate, where he paused. She thought he was coming over to see her and, dashing to the front door she opened it and beckoned him.

He looked up at her, seemed about to ignore her, and then she called, "I've got something to show you, John. Could you very kindly spare me a minute?"

John looked back at his house, over at her and then, as she walked down the path towards him, opened his gate and crossed the road. It occurred to her then that maybe he'd been attempting to flit. Why? It was something, she was sure, to do with Helen.

"What is it Muriel?" he asked peremptorily.

"I've got something to show you."

"What is it?"

"Come and see." She beckoned enticingly and, not attempting to disguise his irritation, he followed her into the house and to the sitting room, where she pointed to the cat curled up on a rug on the sofa. Fond as she felt herself becoming of Skittles, she didn't want her scratching all the furniture, covering it with hairs.

"Skittles?" John said with a note of surprise.

"Yes she's come back."

"Well I never." His voice full of wonderment he went over to her and held out his hand. "When was this?"

"A couple of days ago. I wanted to tell you but . . ." she looked meaningfully in the direction of his house, "you were away."

"I've been away on business," he said.

"I see. John what *is* going on opposite? Is it rude of me to ask? I don't want to be nosy, but—"

"It's not my *wife* they're looking for Muriel if that's what you're thinking," he said rudely. "They are looking for the woman who lived there before. Apparently no one has seen her since and her relatives think, or seem to think, that her husband has done away with her and . . ." he was looking intently at the cat who was now staring at him, eyeball to eyeball, "this cat isn't Skittles."

"But it is," Muriel protested indignantly.

"No it isn't. Look," he bent down and took the cat's chin between his finger and thumb, "this isn't Skittles. It's like her, but the expression is different. So are the markings. This cat shows no recognition of me either. Until the episode with Alan, Skittles and I always got on rather well."

"Perhaps she's afraid of you."

205

"It's not her I tell you."

The cat had risen and prepared to jump down on to the floor.

"But she was in your garden," Muriel spluttered.

John looked at his watch.

"I must go now Muriel," he said, "the police will be wondering what's happened to me. Look, while this investigation is going on I'll be staying at a hotel in town."

"I'll take care of the cat."

"But I tell you it's *not* our cat." He stared at her aggressively. "Do you think I wouldn't know my own cat? Skittles was a deeper grey, with slightly different markings, also a bit smaller."

"But she *answers* to Skittles."

"She's having you on . . . or perhaps she was Skittles in another manifestation," John said with a sarcastic smile. "Helen always thought the place was haunted." Then he turned on his heel, left the house and went swiftly up the garden path without another word.

And she had forgotten all about asking for Pauline's number.

She looked doubtfully at the cat who had changed its mind about leaving – perhaps because John had gone – and was settling down to sleep again.

What could she tell Helen now?

Muriel spent the following two days glued to the window, as discreetly as she could, sitting far back in the corner with the cat on her knee so that she couldn't be seen. The cat seemed very fond of her and she was fond of it. And it was true that Skittles had never been very friendly towards her. But which cat had snarled at her in the wood? Impossible to say.

But in a way it was a relief to know that there now was a real possibility that there had been two tabby cats that looked alike even if they were not identical. Naturally,

John should know. But this cat, her cat, she still addressed as Skittles, had been in the Tempest garden and even now she made a habit of going over every day to wander around. Probably do her business and just sit.

Muriel knew very little about animals, had never owned one or wanted to, and now here she was looking after what she thought was an abandoned cat which was apparently turning out to be a stray.

Very vexing. Very puzzling. What on earth would she do with the cat if she moved?

Then, three days after the original arrival of the police, the fun really began. It started at about seven in the morning with a couple of lorries lumbering up the hill and stationing themselves outside number fourteen. There were about half a dozen men in boiler suits, some lifting gear, digging equipment and blue and white tape with which they proceeded to rope off the house. By this time the village of Tip Hollow was gaining an unwelcome notoriety, and a few stragglers from the village and maybe from outside hung around watching the proceedings from the safety of the road.

Muriel, armed with coffee and sandwiches, didn't miss a thing. After all, these things did happen in real life. It wasn't so long ago since the whole nation had been privy to a series of diggings in and around a house and garden in Gloucester when not one body but about twelve were discovered.

Who in a hundred years could ever have imagined a thing like that? It made the disappearance of Mrs Becket seem small beer in comparison.

Of course the garden of the Tempests' house wasn't very big. But neither had the garden been in Gloucestershire. Muriel was fascinated by the meticulous way the police went about their macabre business, first sectioning off a bit and then proceeding to excavate it with admirable thoroughness.

Well it was *one* way to get the garden turned over, she thought to herself with a wry smile.

On the second day of the dig Muriel took up her usual position in the corner of the sitting room and looked around for the cat. No Skittles in her usual place. She'd given her breakfast so knew she was about. She called for the cat but she didn't come. She went into the back garden and hunted around in the front. No Skittles.

Then she looked across to number fourteen and saw Skittles sitting in the middle of a freshly dug patch of topsoil, just sitting and gazing around her as though she had all the time in the world, a typical Skittles-like attitude. It seemed to amuse one of the policemen who bent down and spoke to her, but she gave him a glance of disdain and then lay down on the ground, turning round several times as if she was on the point of taking a nap.

The policeman tried to pick up the cat but she resisted him, evidently scratching him, because he looked annoyed and shook his hand as though it hurt. Muriel hurried out across the road and called out over the tape.

"I'm so sorry, officer. Can I take her from you?"

"Is this your cat, madam?" the injured policeman called out in a far from friendly tone.

Muriel looked nonplussed. "Not really. I'm just looking after it."

"Then whose cat is it, madam? We can't have it interfering with our operations."

"It's the cat belonging to the house," Muriel said firmly. "It's the Tempests' cat." After all she didn't know for sure it wasn't.

"Oh!" Now it was the turn of the policeman to look nonplussed and he consulted *sotto voce* with a colleague. Then he looked across at Muriel, his expression conciliatory. "Do you think you would be *very kind*, madam, and take the cat into your house?"

"Of course," Muriel said bending down and enticingly holding her hand out to Skittles. But Skittles wouldn't budge.

"Why don't you dig where she's sitting?" Muriel said with a flash of insight she could never afterwards explain. "After all, cats are intuitive. She may know something you don't."

And that, indeed, was where much later in the day they found the bones buried seven feet beneath the topsoil.

The telephone rang quite stridently giving her a shock. The find was on the local news but not the national. It didn't begin to compare with that business in Gloucestershire to figure nationally.

"Muriel?"

"Oh *Helen* . . . at last," Muriel gasped. "I've been wanting to ring you for ages and ages."

"I'm sorry I haven't been in touch." Helen's voice sounded strained, as well it might. "Such a lot has been happening."

"Don't I know it . . . and now they've found the bones."

"Yes, horrible isn't it? It showed there was something all the time, some reason for what was happening in the house. I'm convinced of that. However that isn't all Muriel . . ." Helen paused. "John's been arrested."

"John has been *arrested* . . ." Muriel could hardly contain her amazement.

"Oh nothing to do with that. John has been embezzling the company, Muriel. Quite a large sum of money. There has been an awful lot about John that I knew absolutely nothing about. I feel shell-shocked."

"I can *imagine!*" Muriel's voice was vibrant with sympathy. "I'm so sorry. Helen about the cat—"

"Oh she's fine," Helen said.

"She's with you?"

"As right as rain. She just appeared the moment we were about to get into the taxi. I'm terribly sorry. I know I should have rung you."

Muriel sat looking at the cat which she now knew for certain wasn't Skittles. She didn't know now what to call it and, in a peculiar way, she no longer felt so fond of it. Since the discovery of the bones the cat seemed to have assumed a new dimension. There was something, she thought, other-worldly about the cat, or maybe that was her, by now, rampant imagination.

She hoped to leave very soon, even if she couldn't sell her house and now, with all this fuss opposite, a buyer would probably not be forthcoming for a long while; but still she was determined to go. With a grisly murder opposite, her nerves were all shot to pieces. Ralph Becket had been arrested and taken into custody in wherever it was he now lived, somewhere in the north.

Whatever had happened to anyone else, Muriel also was no longer the person she had been a year before. Not by a long chalk.

In no time at all the garden opposite was put straight, the blue and white police band disappeared and so did all the equipment and traffic and personnel, though a policeman remained on duty at the gate, barring the way. A few stragglers still hung around goggling; but they soon disappeared once there was nothing to see.

Skittles disappeared too, or whatever the cat was. Skittles' *doppelganger*, as Muriel would always think of her as, but also there was a certain sense of relief that she was no longer there. An itinerant cat who probably by now had moved on to a place where she felt more welcome and where her past wasn't known.

Muriel decided it was time to plan her move and a few days later went to see Mr Carr, asking him what chance there was of selling the house in the present market.

Mr Carr shook his head.

"Not much at the moment I'm afraid, Miss Forbes, what with this business and the fact that the market as a whole is sluggish. Of course you might possibly be able to let it."

"Do you think I could?" Muriel looked dubious.

"Oh yes. No problem. Why not?"

"Just *because* of that business opposite."

"People soon forget."

"What will happen to the Tempest house?"

"Now that will be hard to sell, although there are some ghouls about as I don't need to tell you. I hear, however, that it may be repossessed because now that Tempest's lost his job he can't keep up with the mortgage."

"I can't get over him being a gambler. He was always so *mean*. Wouldn't buy his wife a cheap car."

"Well he had to be mean to finance his habit didn't he?" Mr Carr shook his head. "I'm afraid he was a man who was not very popular in the locality. Not much missed I'd say, in the business community. Oh by the way," he looked at her across his desk, "you remember you were interested in who had lived at number fourteen?"

"Well it's not of much consequence now."

"But I thought you'd like to know – and, I say, this *is* a coincidence – my father told me that when the estate was being built the building supervisor disappeared and was never seen or heard of again. Dad didn't think anything more of it until this business cropped up. His name was Anthony Markham and his mother lived in the village."

The woman got off the plane, paused, smiled at assembled cameramen and then gave a short press conference. Now this *was* news, and it made the nationals.

"I only heard that my husband had been arrested a few days ago," she said speaking into a battery of microphones. "I got in touch with the police immediately."

"But why didn't you get in touch before, Mrs Becket?"

211

"Because I wanted to start a new life. Begin all over again."

"But didn't you think that he, and your family, especially your children, would be very worried . . . ?"

Mrs Becket paused. Muriel, who scarcely remembered her, thought she looked an ignorant kind of woman, one who would not really know the effect her actions might have on other people or, possibly, care. She had a selfish sort of mouth and a mulish expression. Maybe she had enjoyed hurting them, and the torment her husband must have suffered when he was arrested for her murder.

"The police said they already knew the bones were old and also that they were those of a man and not a woman," Mrs Becket went on petulantly. "But they withheld the information to try and flush me out. They succeeded. But now that my husband is cleared I intend to return to Canada and resume my new life."

"No chance of a reconciliation with your husband, Mrs Becket?"

"None at all. The past is past and I'm going straight back to Canada just as soon as I can."

The BBC reporter who had intervened turned his face to camera.

"Then whose bones are they which have languished for so long in the garden of a house on a hill in west Dorset?"

Muriel thought she knew.

Epilogue

The house stood neglected, waiting for a buyer. But even though it was repossessed, going very cheaply, no one was interested, not even those ghoulish members of the public who enjoyed disasters. Perhaps it was out of fear that the ghost of Anthony Markham, who had disappeared thirty years before, still lingered; or perhaps it was simply because no one wanted to live in a house near the spot from which the soul of a man had for so many years cried to heaven for vengeance.

For Anthony Markham had been murdered, his skull caved in with a blunt instrument, his body buried beneath builders' rubble. After thirty years it was doubtful if his killer would ever be found though, as was their duty, the police wearily took up another case of skulduggery that went back a generation and offered no clues. They probably knew the futility of trying to trace scores of itinerant building workers, now dispersed throughout the country, and find one who once had a grudge against an unpopular supervisor.

Rumours in the village at the time apparently speculated that Markham's disappearance was an attempt to escape the clutches of an overpossessive mother, and begin a new life.

John Tempest was eventually jailed for three years for embezzlement, but released after two for good behaviour. Like many convicts before him he went to Australia in an attempt to forget the past.

Helen Tempest continued to live for some time with

her friend Pauline. Eventually she got a flat in her beloved Worcester Park where she and her two children, together with the cat Skittles, settled down happily, glad to be back in a civilized place.

Muriel Forbes rented a bungalow on the south coast. Her house opposite number fourteen Tip Hollow Hill was rented by a professional working couple who had no imagination at all, and were probably the best tenants she could have hoped for.

In the churchyard of the village of Tip Hollow, the grave of Rita Markham was only temporarily disturbed to make way for the remains of her long-forgotten son, Anthony, who she probably loved as much as any mother loves any son, and doubtlessly mourned to the end of her days.

Now, united at last, they lie side by side.

Momentarily Tip Hollow was in the news but, as a topic of interest, it rapidly faded and was soon forgotten as other, even more frightful global events of mayhem and slaughter took its place.

Sometimes at night the wind soughs in the trees as if sighing sadly over the grave, and sometimes a grey feline is seen sitting at the base of the cross surmounting it.

And then it seems to vanish, creeping stealthily through the undergrowth as silently and as surreptitiously as it came.